We Cry Tomorrow

James S. Roodhouse

VANTAGE PRESS
New York

Published by Vantage Press, Inc.
516 West 34th Street, New York, New York 10001

Manufactured in the United States of America
ISBN: 0-533-12471-9

Library of Congress Catalog Card No.: 97-90799

0 9 8 7 6 5 4 3 2 1

To my wife, Rosa Lee, who has always encouraged me

1

Lane Streeter pulled the big gate shut, slid the bar into place, and turned to his companion.

"Well, there's another day finished, Renny. Come on over to the house and I'll pay you now. This is the end of the month, you know."

"Okay, Lane," the young fellow replied. "I'll pick up some groceries on the way home."

They walked over to the big, comfortable ranch house where Lane opened the door to the room that served as his office, seated himself, and beckoned Renny to another chair. Lane wrote out a check, blew it dry, and handed it to Renny.

"Lane, this is too much; this is for thirty-five dollars instead of thirty," said Renny.

"That's okay, you earned it," replied Lane. "That's hard work keeping tabs on that many horses."

They had just returned from shipping fifty horses by rail to a large ranch in Kansas.

"Well, thanks, Lane, I really appreciate it. Maybe I'll get a small present for Mom with the extra," Renny said.

"Okay, Renny, I'll see you Monday then. Don't forget we have those twenty horses for John Redfield," said Lane.

After Renny had left, Lane walked through the house into the kitchen where his mother, Martha Streeter, was busy baking pies. "Any coffee left, Mom?" asked Lane.

"There should be," she replied. "Get all your horses shipped?"

"Yeah, they're all gone. You know, Mom, Renny is a good worker. I gave him an extra five dollars. I think he earned it," Lane said.

"Son, I'm glad you did. He's the breadwinner in that family now that his dad is dead."

Lane poured himself a cup of coffee. "Where's Callie?" he asked.

"She's spending the afternoon with Charity Grissom. She should be home anytime now. Lane, will you please hitch up Nellie to the buggy?" Martha asked. "Callie and I are going to town to do some shopping. Do you want to go with us?"

"I'm going in to see if Mr. Gomez has those bridles ready yet, but I'm going to ride Midnight; he needs the exercise."

"We won't be ready for about a half hour," said Martha.

"Okay, Mom, just holler when you're ready."

Lane walked back to his office, sipping his coffee. He leaned back in his chair with his hands locked behind his head. He began to reminisce about the last nine years of his life.

It would be nine years in May since his dad, Morgan Streeter, had been killed. He had been shot in the back by parties unknown. Morg Streeter had always loved horses. Two years after he had been appointed sheriff, he had purchased the land and started a horse ranch. He had never had the time to really build the business due to his commitment as sheriff. Some said that Morg Streeter was the fastest gunman of all time. He had been sheriff of Craver County for twelve years at the time of his death. He had completely cleaned up the county in two short years.

Lane could remember the day they brought his dad home. His grief had been almost unbearable.

Cappy Swinson, an old former cowpuncher his dad

had working for him, had more or less taken over and kept things going. Lane was sixteen when Cappy died. Against his mother's objections, Lane had quit school and had taken command. His mother had thought he was too young, but Lane knew more about horses than many older men. His dad had taught him all he knew, which was considerable.

Lane's thoughts came back to the present. He had made a go of it. Today, for example, he had banked a check for five thousand dollars. He had another thousand horses that he and Renny had captured. He had a way with animals. They seemed to know that he was their friend.

Lane was now nineteen, but most people thought he was older. Few people knew it, but Lane was very strong. He had started a practice when he was only nine of picking up a tiny colt. Every day he would pick the colt up and show his dad. When the colt got larger and he could still lift it, his dad realized that Lane was unusually strong. After his dad's death, Land discontinued the practice. His dad had also schooled him in the use of a gun.

"Lane, a gun is a tool," Morg told his son. "Never use a gun carelessly. Use it only if you must."

The only person who knew of his skill with a gun was the town doctor. Doctor Baldwin had called at the house one day when Callie, Lane's younger sister, was sick, and, unbeknown to Lane, had seen him practicing.

"That boy is another Morg Streeter all over again," mused Doc aloud to himself.

Lane was bigger than his dad had been, standing six feet three and weighing nearly two hundred pounds. As he pondered his present situation, he realized how much his success was due to his father's training. The ranch was doing very well, with the horse market in high demand.

Cappy Swinson had also helped, advising him about breeding practices and the care of animals. Because of that, he now had one hundred head of really good horses that would bring a high price on the market. Several of his horses he would never sell, foremost of which was Midnight, the huge, black stallion he had caught two years before. It had taken Lane more than a year to train the horse exactly the way he wanted. Now, he was the only person who could ride Midnight. John Redfield, who had the largest cattle ranch in the territory, had offered him one thousand dollars for Midnight, but Lane refused to sell him.

Looking out the window, Lane saw Callie ride in and he knew his mother would be wanting to leave soon. He went out to the small barn where his mother's horse, Nellie, was kept, and hitched her to the buggy. He then went over to the big barn where Midnight was kept. The giant horse nickered playfully and nuzzled Lane's cheek. Lane affectionately petted his nuzzle and scratched him behind the ears.

"Ready to take a run, big fellow?" Lane asked.

He led the horse over to where his mother and Callie were already in the buggy.

"See you in town later," he said. "I'll treat you to dinner with one condition."

"What's that?" Martha asked.

"That we eat dessert at home," he said. "I saw those pies you baked." His mother smiled, "All right; that's a bargain."

He mounted and guided Midnight down the lane and onto the main road.

2

Haleyville, Arizona, was a town of about one thousand residents. It was named after its founder, Thomas Haley, said to be the first citizen who appeared on the scene. After Morg Streeter's death, the town council had appointed Josh Cantwell as sheriff. He was a short, heavy-set man in his late forties. He was slow to think, slow to move, but very thorough. He was seated outside his office, soaking up the late afternoon sun when he saw Lane Streeter riding past on a huge black horse.

"Hi, boy," he said, "how's the horse business going?"

"Oh, kicking along." Lane smiled. "What's new with you, Mr. Cantwell?"

"Same old thing, son; nothing ever happens here anymore."

Morg Streeter and Josh Cantwell had been close friends, and Sheriff Cantwell had a lot of respect for Lane. He marveled at the way Lane had taken over a tough business and had made a growing success out of it.

"What are you riding there, son? Is that a horse or an elephant?"

"This is my pet colt, Midnight; he's kind of puny right now, but when he grows up, he'll fill out a little more," said Lane.

"I'd hate to pay his food bills," said Sheriff Cantwell, laughing.

"He does eat quite a bit for a fact," said Lane. "Well, see you later, Sheriff. I have to see Mr. Gomez."

Lane went on down the street and pulled up in front of a sign that read 'Gomez Leather Works,' tied up to the hitch rail, and went inside.

5

"Hi, Mr. Gomez, are my bridles ready?" asked Lane.

"Hello, Lane, Yes, they are all finished," said Mr. Gomez.

Lane examined the bridles and found them to be excellent.

"You have magic in those fingers of yours, Mr. Gomez," said Lane.

"You work magic with horses; my talent is in leather," said Mr. Gomez. "I wish I could handle horses like you."

"Well, what are the damages this time?" asked Lane. "I suppose it will be a fortune again," he said, smiling.

"Only one million dollars," Mr. Gomez said, laughing. "After all, you are my very good friend."

"Oh, good, you've lowered your prices."

Mr. Gomez laughed uproariously. "You should come in here more often; you liven things up when you come in. No, the price is the same as before: four dollars apiece."

Lane paid his bill and said, "I'll probably have some more work for you soon."

"Anytime for you, Lane, you know that."

Lane left the shop and stepped outside. There he saw several men gathered around Midnight. One man in particular was trying to untie the horse from the hitch rail; Midnight was rolling his eyes and was very restless.

"Get away from that horse!" yelled Lane. "Are you trying to get yourself killed?"

"Don't get so mouthy, kid," said the man. He was a very stocky man, with huge arms, an immense chest and broad shoulders.

"I'm only trying to save your life, friend. That horse could kill you," said Lane.

"He was only looking him over because he was thinking of buying him," spoke up another man.

"Okay, but he's not for sale, not at any price," said Lane.

"Let's go, Jorms," said his companion.

"Wait a minute. I don't like anyone talking to me like that!" snarled Jorms. "That kid has a big mouth and I aim to close it!"

"But not now, Jorms. Besides, he's not the one." Leading Jorms aside, he whispered something in his ear.

"Okay, okay, Lefty," said Jorms. "But I'll be seeing you again, kid, and don't you forget it!"

The two men turned and walked down the street.

Ed Landers, who ran the general store, said, "Lane, are you trying to get yourself killed? That guy would eat you alive!"

"I appreciate your concern, Ed, but I don't think there's any cause for worry," said Lane.

Sheriff Cantwell, noticing the commotion, had come down from his office to see what was going on.

"Any problems, Lane?" he asked.

"Nothing serious," said Lane. "But I wonder what that Lefty meant by saying 'he's not the one.'"

"What could he mean by that?" asked the sheriff.

"Well, I'm not going to worry about it," responded Lane.

3

John and Abby Mason had set out for California more than thirty years ago, determined to find a new life in a new land. The wagon train had been attacked by Indians, and, along with some other families, the Masons had been separated from the train. They stopped over in Haleyville to rest and decided to try the food at the only restaurant in town. The food, in Abby's words, was next to impossible. Deciding to do something about it, the Masons opened their own eating place and soon drove the other restaurant out of business. They then decided to stay in Haleyville, and, being fairly well-to-do, they had a hotel built, along with a large dining room. With the growth of the town, which had expanded from two hundred residents to one thousand, they had prospered and found that this was where they wanted to stay forever.

They were well liked and had some very close friends, among whom were Morg and Martha Streeter and their children. When Morg Streeter had been brought home dead, Abby immediately went out to the Streeter ranch and stayed several days. Recognizing the depth of Lane's grief, Abby had taken him in her arms and consoled him the best she could.

"Lane, I know you loved your dad and you will miss him terribly in these next few months, but he would not want you to quit living and just give up," she said. "Life must go on and we will cry in some of those tomorrows also, but you will find that life is good if we do our part to make it so."

She realized that she loved these children as if they had been her own. She and John had never had any children, much to their regret. She was proud when Lane had taken over the operation of the ranch at such an early age and made a smashing success of it.

It was nearly five o'clock when Lane, his mother and sister walked into the dining room.

"I'm so hungry I could eat a horse!" exclaimed Lane, and seeing Abby nearby, he added, "If we eat here, we may have to."

"Oh, you young scamp, just sit down and be quiet for a change," Abby said. "You have had only good food here and you know it!"

"I don't know," said Lane. "Little Billy Parker was telling me that his dog ate some food you put out for him and he died."

"Martha, why don't you get a hobble for his mouth, or at least do something to shut him up?" Abby said, laughing.

Just then John Mason walked into the dining room, and hearing the last part of their badinage, asked, "Is she picking on you again, Lane? She does the same to me."

"Yeah, she won't let me alone. A body comes in here to have a peaceful meal and what happens? Yak, yak, yak, that's all I hear," said Lane, laughing.

"Oh, go along with you both; one is as bad as the other," said Abby, smiling.

The other patrons were enjoying this humorous byplay, having heard it before. One of them picked up on it now: "Lane, the other day she served me some fish and I started to eat it, and the bobber was still in it."

"Oh, Ed Landers, you're as bad as he is!" Abby laughingly exclaimed, as she headed for the kitchen.

"Lane, I think it's terrible the way you tease Aunt Abby," said Callie.

"Abby doesn't mind; in fact, she enjoys it," said Martha.

After a most delicious meal, the Streeters left the dining room, heading for home. Lane loved this part of the day, with the softening shadows and dusk stealing in. The smell of the sage, the cooling breezes were like an elixir to him.

"I could spend the rest of my life here in this land," mused Lane as he rode along. "God has certainly been good to me." When he got back to the ranch, he put Midnight in the barn, threw down some hay for the animals, and went into the house.

4

Four men sat around a table in a little cabin about twenty miles from Haleyville. The leader of the men had papers in front of him on which a map of sorts had been drawn.

"Boys, we have to make sure that everything is planned out to a tee. We don't want anything to go wrong at this stage of the game," he said. "Lefty Bowens and Lee Jorms are in Haleyville now. Jorms will take care of Tom Redfield. Lefty is making sure we have everything covered."

"What made you pick Haleyville for our next job?" asked one of the men.

"Figger it out for yourself, Hank. Morg Streeter kept a lid on that town for all these years. Nobody ever thinks of anything happening there. But Morg Streeter's dead now. What better place to pick?" said the Boss.

"Is there money in that bank?" asked another man.

"This is where having an inside man comes in handy, Bill," said the boss. "Our man tells me that at the end of every month there is about two hundred fifty thousand dollars plus a number of gold bars from the Big Top Mine. It will be like taking candy from a baby."

"Wait a minute, Brady, wait a minute," said the fourth member of the group. "You forget I'm new in these parts. Why don't you start at the beginning and clue me in?"

"You're right, Boley. Tell you what, why don't you ask questions about our setup, and I'll do my best to answer them," said Brady.

"Now you're talking, Brady," said Boley. "First of all, you said Jorms would take care of this Tom Redfield, whoever he is."

11

"Tom Redfield is the oldest son of John Redfield, the biggest rancher in that area. Tom is about the toughest guy around and is about the only one around who might give us trouble," said Brady.

"What about the sheriff, or don't they have a sheriff?" asked Boley.

"Yeah, they have a sheriff, but I've taken care of that. When the holdup is going on, he'll be down in the lower end of the county. By the time he gets back, we'll be long gone," explained Brady.

"Hey, that's slick!" exclaimed Boley. "But what about that John Redfield; don't he count for anything?"

"Redfield's an old man; he has three other sons, but they won't bother us none. No, Tom is the only one who could put a crimp in our plans, and he won't be able to, once Jorms gets through with him," said Brady.

"How's he going to do that?" asked Hank.

"Why, he's going to beat him up so bad that he won't be able to get around for a few days," said Brady.

"Will Jorms be able to do it, if this Tom is so tough?" asked Boley.

"You sure don't know Jorms or you wouldn't ask that," put in Bill.

"Nobody has ever whipped Jorms; sometimes I think he is more animal that man. I sure wouldn't want him after me," said Brady. "His only problem is that he is stupid; that's why Lefty is with him, to keep him in line."

"What about this Streeter guy; didn't he have any brothers or anyone who could cause us trouble?" asked Boley.

"Nope, no brothers, only a son, but he's only nineteen; nothing to worry about there," said Brady.

"Well, how are we going to work it then? What is your plan?" again asked Boley. "I'm sorry to ask so many questions, Brady, but I was in a holdup once where no plans had been made, and I wound up doing ten years in jail."

"That's okay, Boley, that's what we want. The more questions, the better. We sure don't want any loopholes now," said Brady. "To be safe, Lefty and Jorms are going to set an old building on fire at the edge of town to draw all the people away from the center of town."

"Boy, you've thought of everything, haven't you? That's the way I like it!" said Boley admiringly.

"Everybody satisfied then?" asked Brady. "We don't want any slip-ups."

"What date have you picked for the job?" asked Hank.

"This is nearly the end of March; we'll put it on April 29th; that will be a Saturday," said Brady. "Hank, you and Bill come in from the east end of town and Boley and me will come in from the west. It won't hurt if you ask if anyone is hiring riders in case people get suspicious."

"One last question, Brady," said Boley. "What time of day do we pull the holdup?"

"We generally pull all our jobs around ten o'clock in the morning; most of the early customers are out of the bank by then," said Brady.

"One other thing, Brady," said Hank. "You say Lefty and Jorms won't be riding out of town with us?"

"No, they won't be suspected of being with us; they'll meet us later back here at the hideout," replied Brady. "One last thing, boys, keep out of trouble 'til we meet. Okay?"

5

Morg and Martha Streeter had raised their children in the church, so, on this Sunday morning, the Streeter family was on the way to church.

"Maybe if you are lucky, Lane, the Holidays will be in church and you will get to see Elaine," teased Callie.

"Well, I hope so," said Lane. "By the way, Renny told me he and his mother were going, so that should make you happy."

Callie's face reddened and she said, "Oh, I don't care a hoot about Renny Barker."

"That's strange," said Lane. "Yesterday before we drove the horses into town, Renny was sure some kind of thirsty and had to keep going to the house for a drink of water. I wonder why after you left for Grissoms' he wasn't thirsty anymore."

"Oh, you are just making that up!" said Callie, now thoroughly red in the face.

By now they were at the church, so Lane dropped them in front of the church, parked the buggy at the hitch rack, tied up Nellie, and joined Martha and Callie in their pew. The church was nearly filled. Lane looked around, seeking a certain familiar face. He found her sitting with the rest of the Holiday family. He waved at her and got an answering wave in return.

The Reverend Robert Manning had come to pastor the Haleyville Methodist Church five years ago and was a big favorite with nearly all the people. He was not only an astute student of the Bible, but a student of people also. Lane had heard his mother say once, "I wouldn't want to tell him a lie while he was looking me in the eye."

Reverend Manning now took his place behind the pulpit.

"Let us now quiet our minds and worship the Lord," said Reverend Manning.

He then led the congregation in two hymns and asked if there were any prayer requests. Hearing none, he then led the congregation in prayer. He had a strong authoritative voice. His prayer was simple, asking God to meet the needs of the congregation, and to draw the people closer to Him.

He then announced to the congregation his sermon text. "My text for this morning's message is the first verse in the fourteenth chapter of the Gospel of John, 'Let not your heart be troubled: ye believe in God, believe also in Me'."

He went on to tell the people about many of the promises of God, that He was able to fulfill those promises if the people had faith to believe and trust Him. He spoke for about thirty minutes and was getting ready to close his sermon when a large dog entered the sanctuary, walked up and sat in front of the altar. Several of the children snickered and even some of the adults had a hard time keeping a straight face.

Never at a loss for words, Reverend Manning, also seeing the humor of the situation, asked, "Are there any other seekers?" Everyone laughed and then Reverend Manning dismissed with prayer.

While shaking hands at the door, Lane smiled and said, "I wondered how you would handle that situation, Pastor; that was quick thinking."

"Thank you, Lane," Reverend Manning said. "I'm sure God has a sense of humor, too, and I believe He wants us to laugh occasionally." Lane now sought out Elaine Holiday. "My, oh my, some people just get prettier

15

every time I see them."

Blushing prettily, Elaine said, "I didn't know you looked at so many girls to see how pretty they looked."

Elaine Holiday was a very pretty, young lady. She had dark brown hair, was five feet four, and had a very sunny disposition. She was extremely fond of Lane and everyone took for granted that they would some day tie the knot. Her father, Bob Holiday, ran a large farm on which he grew many varieties of vegetables. He was the main supplier for many of the townspeople and the stores and restaurants.

"How about me driving over this afternoon and you and me going for a buggy ride?" asked Lane.

"That sounds like a good idea to me," responded Elaine. "What time?"

"Oh, about two-thirty or thereabouts," said Lane. "I'll be ready," she replied.

As they drove home, Callie again began teasing Lane. "I noticed that you talked to Miss Wonderful. What have you planned for today?" she asked.

"We're planning a buggy ride. Why, did you and Renny want to go along?" Lane asked.

"Oh, Mom, make him stop it!" she exclaimed, her face rosy red.

"I think you are both being very foolish," said Martha.

"Mom, you're forgetting something, aren't you?" Lane asked. "What's that?" asked Martha.

"I can remember when I was small, and I would see Dad kissing you," he answered.

"Well, that was different; we were married," she answered.

"Are you telling me that you never kissed Dad before you were married?" asked Lane.

"Oh, you two drive a body to distraction!" she

16

exclaimed, and now her face was red. "Seriously, though, Lane, are you and Elaine figuring on getting married soon?"

"No, Mom, we both think we are too young; we have our whole lives ahead of us and we both think there's plenty of time," said Lane.

"How old were you and Dad when you got married, Mom?" asked Callie.

"Your dad was twenty-four, and I was twenty-two," answered Martha.

"Callie was hoping you would say you were fifteen," said Lane, smiling.

"Oh, I was not!" retorted Callie.

By now they were at home once more, so Lane put the horse and buggy away while Martha and Callie started preparing dinner.

*　　*　　*

At precisely two-thirty, Lane arrived at the Holiday farm. True to her word, Elaine was ready to go. Lane helped her into the buggy and started out the lane to the main road.

"Anywhere in particular, or just drive around?" he asked.

"Let's go up to Sentinel Rock," she said.

Sentinel Rock was one of the highest points around, and many people would go there to look down on the scenery. They drove up to the Rock, got out and seated themselves on the ground.

"Lane, something happened yesterday that bothered me," said Elaine.

"What was that?" asked Lane.

"I was hanging up clothes yesterday morning when

two men rode past. They saw me and came over and asked if they could water their horses. One of the men was the biggest man I have ever seen," said Elaine. "He just gave me the shivers the way he looked at me and made some remark about seeing me later."

"You never saw them before?" asked Lane.

"No, they were strangers to me," she said. "And, really, the other man didn't say much, but the large man just turned me cold."

"It may have been the same two men that I had a little set-to with in town," said Lane. "He was fooling around with Midnight, and I yelled at him to get away from Midnight, and he got very upset. He told me he would see me later. The other man whispered something to him and then made some remark about me not being the one, and then they walked down the street somewhere. Sheriff Cantwell and I were wondering what he meant by me not being the one."

"That is strange," said Elaine. "I hope I never see that man again."

"The big man's name is Jorms; at least that's what the other one called him. The other man's name was Lefty," said Lane. "I think those two will bear watching."

"Lane, I don't want you having any trouble with them," said Elaine. "That big man looked like he could whip a whole army by himself."

"Well, honey, we just have to take what comes; and that big man just might run into a surprise," said Lane.

"What do you mean, a surprise?" she asked.

"Oh, nothing much, just a small surprise," said Lane.

They got back into the buggy, drove around for a few hours, and Lane dropped her off at her home.

"This is the part I like best," said Lane, laughingly, as he drew her to him and kissed her.

"Oh, you!" she exclaimed. "Lane, promise me you'll be careful."

"I'm always careful," he said, smiling at her. "I'll see you in a few days."

As he pulled away, he looked back. She blew him a kiss. He did likewise and drove on home.

"What a wonderful girl," he mused. "Lord, thank you for bringing her into my life."

6

The next morning Lane and Renny rounded up the twenty horses that Lane had promised John Redfield. They were out of the one hundred that Lane had gentled completely and were now ready for use in rounding up cattle. They were excellent cutting horses and were sound in every feature. Lane had always believed in selling only quality animals, and these were some of the best.

"There comes Mr. Redfield and his riders now," said Renny. John Redfield had four sons, Tom, Phil, Andy, and Wayne, and they were all with him now.

"'Lo, Lane," said Tom, smiling. "I suppose these are all culls."

"Yep, just like the last time," said Lane, laughing. "After all, I don't get too many people I can palm these off on."

"Well, Lane, I wish everybody would cheat me the same way you do," said John. "Those last horses I got from you were some of the best horses I have every owned. I'll repeat my offer for Midnight."

"Sorry, Mr. Redfield, but I just can't bring myself to part with him. He's the most horse I've ever owned," said Lane.

"Lane, how fast can that horse run?" asked Andy.

"Well, I'll tell you, Andy," said Lane with a twinkle in his eye, "one time I left here for town at ten o'clock, I arrived in town at ten 'til ten."

A roar of laughter went up. "Well, that's pretty fast all right," said John. "Well, boys, what say we get these animals home?"

He extended a check to Lane.

"Thank you, Mr. Redfield," said Lane. "It's a pleasure doing business with you."

"The pleasure's all mine, boy," said John, as they headed down the lane for home.

"Lane, when will you start letting me break the horses the way you do?" asked Renny.

"When you're a little older, Renny. What would I do if you broke a bone or something worse?" asked Lane. "I would have to hire another man to help me. Where could I get another worker who knows as much as you do about the job? Besides, if you got hurt, Callie would tear me apart."

"Oh, you're just saying that!" blurted Renny, somewhat mollified by Lane's explanation. "But, say, Callie sure is a swell girl."

"Yeah, she's my favorite sister," said Lane, laughing.

For the next three weeks, Lane and Renny were very busy, gentling more horses and occasionally catching more. One morning Lane went out to the large enclosure where they kept the majority of the horses.

"Let's check them over very carefully, Renny, for in this new group will be some culls," said Lane.

"How do you know which ones to let go?" asked Renny.

"I'll show you," said Lane.

They looked over several before they came to one that Lane singled out. "Look here, Renny; see that flat spot on his shoulder? He will have to be let go; that shoulder could give out on him just at a crucial moment, and that could spell trouble for his rider."

"I would never have noticed it if you hadn't called my attention to it," said Renny. "I doubt if anyone else would have either."

"A man who knows horses would know it," said Lane.

"I will never sell a man a horse that isn't in top condition."

"Boy, Lane, I doubt if I can ever learn as much about horses as you," said Renny.

"You will if you keep your eyes open and learn what to look for," said Lane.

They took the rest of the day clearing the rest of the culls and then releasing them back to the wild.

"Lane, I'm curious about something," said Renny.

"What's that, Renny?" asked Lane.

"Take the ones we let go; couldn't their colts have the same problem?" asked Renny.

"No, those problems aren't hereditary," explained Lane. "Those things usually happen from something else; maybe in a fight with another horse a bone could get chipped off or maybe a large rock falling could accidentally hit the horse and maim its shoulder or some other part of its body."

"Oh, I see," said Renny. "Tell me this, Lane, is there anything about horses you don't know?"

Lane laughed. "Renny, you could write a book on what I don't know."

7

Gus Porter was happy. He was the owner and bartender of the Lone Eagle saloon, and it was doing a thriving business on this particular evening. Several customers were at the bar, four other men were in the rear of the building shooting pool, and a friendly poker game was in progress at one of the many card tables. Tom Redfield was teasing Whip Mains about letting Hi Walker bluff him out of the last pot. Whip was the stage driver while Hi owned the livery stable. Along with Ed Landers, they often got together for their round of poker. The stakes were never very high; it was more for fun than anything else.

"Looks like I'm going to lose my shirt again, playing with you three shysters," said Tom, "but that's the way it usually is."

"Listen to that, would you," said Ed, laughing. "And after all the times he's taken us to the cleaners."

"My heart bleeds for him," said Whip.

Just then the door opened and two men entered the room. One was the man called Lefty, and the other was Jorms. They walked up to the bar. Gus wiped the bar in front of them and asked, "What will it be, gents?"

"Just a glass of beer," said Lefty. "What'll you have, Lee?"

"Make mine whiskey," said Jorms.

After looking around the room, Lefty drew Jorms aside and, in a low tone, muttered something to him. With his drink in his hand, Jorms walked over to the poker game and stood watching for a few minutes. Moving over behind Tom's chair, he continued to watch.

"Something you wanted, Mister?" asked Tom.

"Just watching," answered Jorms.

"I don't like people standing in back of me when I'm playing poker," said Tom.

"What's the matter, you afraid I'll catch you cheating?" asked Jorms, in a sneering manner.

A hush fell over those watching; this was a deliberate insult. One man never accused another man of cheating unless he caught him at it and was prepared to back it up.

"Mister, I'll give you ten seconds to apologize for that remark!" retorted Tom.

"If you don't like it, you know what you can do about it!" snarled Jorms.

Tom rose to his feet and turned to face Jorms. Jorms immediately put his fists up and moved toward Tom.

"Just a moment, gents," said Gus, brandishing a shotgun. "I don't want any trouble in here; take your argument outside."

"You're right, Gus," said Tom. "Mister, I don't know what this is all about, but you either apologize or else."

"Apologize nothing, you lousy four-flusher. I'm going to enjoy taking you apart!" said Jorms.

They all walked outside where Tom and Jorms squared off. Tom feinted with the left, and caught Jorms with a solid right cross to the jaw. Jorms only laughed and moved in on Tom. He hit Tom with a left and Tom gasped; he had never been hit that hard in his life. He shot a left and a right in rapid succession with no apparent effect on Jorms. Jorms crowded Tom into the hitch rail and smashed a vicious right to the midsection. Tom doubled up in pain. Jorms brought his right knee up and caught Tom full in the face. By now, Tom's nose and mouth were streaming blood. Jorms hit him again with another punch in the back of the neck. Tom dropped to the ground, moaning softly. Jorms kicked him viciously in the ribs and drew back his leg for another kick, when a voice stopped him.

"There'll be none of that, Mister, he's already down. What are you trying to do, kill him?" Sheriff Cantwell had come up behind the crowd and now stood with his gun in Jorms's ribs.

"Sheriff, you're going to be the sorriest man alive for sticking that gun in my ribs!" snarled Jorms. "Nobody does that to me!"

"And you're going to be dead if you don't back off," said Sheriff Cantwell. "A fair fight is one thing, but it ceased to be a fair fight when you kicked him in the ribs."

"Somebody had better get Doc Baldwin," said Hi Walker, bending over Tom. "He could be hurt pretty bad."

"Come on, Jorms, let's get out of here," said Lefty.

"Not so fast there," said Sheriff Cantwell. "What started all this anyway?"

Everybody started talking at once, causing Sheriff Cantwell to say, "Whoa up, I can't hear everybody at once. Ed, were you there when this started?"

"Yeah, I was, Sheriff, and it looked to me like this man deliberately picked the fight," said Ed. "He—"

"You're a liar!" ejaculated Jorms. "He started it!"

"Sheriff, I don't know what this is all about, but from what I saw, this man was trying to pick a fight," spoke up Whip. "You know as well as I do that a man doesn't stand behind another man when he's playing cards; it's kind of an unwritten rule."

"That's right, Whip," said the sheriff. "And that's what Jorms was doing?"

"He sure was, and when Tom objected to it, this guy got all huffy about it," said Whip. "He even hinted that maybe Tom might be cheating."

"Mister, whoever you are, don't let me catch you

alone!" warned Jorms.

"Jorms, just who do you think you are? Just because a person doesn't agree with your viewpoint on something doesn't give you the right to threaten him. If I hear of you causing trouble over this, I'll throw you in jail so fast your head will swim!" retorted Sheriff Cantwell.

"You can always try, Sheriff," jeered Jorms.

Just then Doc Baldwin appeared. He looked at the figure on the ground and dropped beside him.

"What happened to him?" asked Doc.

"He tried to throw the tough-guy act at me and he got what was coming to him," snarled Jorms. "And the same thing could happen to some more people around here."

"Come on, Lee, let's get out of here," spoke up Lefty.

"That's good advice, fellow, and you would do well to follow it," said Sheriff Cantwell.

"Maybe you're big enough to drive me out, big mouth," said Jorms. "If so, hop to it!"

Doc Baldwin spoke to the men around him. "Will some of you help carry Tom down to my office? I'm afraid he's hurt pretty bad."

Four of the men gathered there stooped down, lifted Tom and carried him away. Lefty and Jorms got on their horses and rode off.

"You know, boys, I always figgered that Tom Redfield was just about the toughest man around these parts, but that fellow handled him like he was a half-grown kid," said the sheriff. "Just a few punches and he was out of it. Make no mistake about it, Mr. Jorms is one tough customer."

"If he tries to make good his threat to me, I'll shoot his heart out!" retorted Whip Mains.

"That may be the only way to handle him; he's about as cross-grained as any person I've ever met," said the sheriff.

8

Lane Streeter was mildly surprised to see Sheriff Cantwell riding up just as Lane was crossing from the barn to the house. "Hi, Sheriff, what brings you out this way?" asked Lane.

"Lane, you remember that fellow Jorms, who was shooting off his mouth in town several weeks ago?" asked Sheriff Cantwell.

"You mean that big guy who was fooling around with Midnight?" asked Lane.

"That's the one. Well, see what you make of this. A couple hours ago in town, he gave Tom Redfield as bad a beating as a man ever got. Four ribs broken and other things. The reason I came out to tell you about it is because of that remark that fellow Lefty made. You remember 'he's not the one'?" said Sheriff Cantwell.

"Oh, yeah," said Lane. "We were wondering what he meant by that remark."

"Well, now he beats up on Tom. Could Tom be 'the one' he was talking about?" asked the sheriff.

"Now you've got me wondering, Sheriff," said Lane. "But what reason could he have for doing what he did? Did he know Tom from before someplace?"

"I talked to Tom afterward, and he said he never saw the man before. He can't figger it out either," said the sheriff. "But Tom is pretty sure that Jorms deliberately started the fight."

"Sheriff, there has to be a reason for it," said Lane. "A man just doesn't pick a fight for something to do."

"You know, son, I didn't think anybody could handle Tom that easily. That Jorms is one rough guy, and he is also very dangerous. He threatened to beat up some of the others there. When I threatened to throw him in jail, he told me to try it," said Sheriff Cantwell.

"Is he crazy or what?" asked Lane. "Sheriff, don't try to arrest him by yourself if it comes to that; get some help from somebody."

"Another thing, son," said the sheriff, "that other man, Lefty, was with him. Well, I looked through my old wanted posters and there he was on one of them. He was wanted for robbery down in Texas years ago."

"Can you throw him in jail on that charge?" asked Lane.

"Well, son, usually when a man comes from another state, we don't bother him unless he starts trouble in our area. Now, if this was recent, that would be different. But this was years ago. Did your dad ever say anything like that?" asked the sheriff.

"I heard him tell Mom something like that, but I was small then and I didn't pay any attention to it," said Lane.

"Well, it gives us something to think about," said the sheriff. "I'll certainly keep my eye on those two."

"Sheriff, I almost forgot; those two men were out at the Holidays' the other day, and they scared the living daylights out of Elaine," said Lane. "I should say the big one did. She said the other man didn't say much."

"What were they doing out there?" asked Sheriff Cantwell.

"They told her they wanted to water their horses," said Lane, "but you know they could have watered their horses anywhere. I'm going to tell you something, Mr. Cantwell, if either of those men bother Elaine, I'm going after them!"

"I know how you feel, son, but don't do anything foolish," said the sheriff. "That big man, Jorms, is a mighty bad actor. Look what he did to Tom."

"Well, I'm not looking for trouble, but I'm not running from it, either," said Lane.

"That's all well and good, Lane, but you let the law handle them," said the sheriff. "Well, I've got to be going; I'll see you later, son."

"So long, Sheriff," said Lane.

9

Bob Holiday walked into the house and spoke to his wife. "Jennie, do you need anything from town? I'm going in to get some more seeds. We're growing more vegetables all the time."

"Dad, can I go in with you?" asked Elaine. "I have to get some dress goods."

"Here's a list of things I need also," said Jennie.

Bob hitched up his buckboard and pulled over in front of the house.

Elaine came running out and got up on the seat beside him. They took off down the lane and headed for town.

"I don't want to stay in town long, honey. How long do you think it will take you?" Bob asked.

"Not long, Dad," she answered. "Not more than fifteen minutes."

"Good," he said. "I've got to get back and get the planting done."

"Oh, look, Dad!" she exclaimed. "There goes Lane way up ahead of us. I'd know that horse anywhere."

"Well, honey, I couldn't catch him if I had to," he said, grinning.

"Oh, Dad, you know I didn't mean for you to catch him," she said, blushing.

When they pulled up in front of Ed Landers's store, they saw Midnight farther down the street, tied to the hitch rack.

"I'm going down to Marge's Dress Shop first, and then I'll meet you in Ed's store," she said.

"Okay, honey, and if you want to, I guess it would be

all right if you saw Lane," he said, snickering.

Marge's Dress Shop was several buildings down the street, next to the hardware store. As Elaine was about to enter the shop, two men came out of the hardware store. They were Lee Jorms and Lefty Bowens.

"Well, look who's here, Lefty, our little friend. Honey, I told you I'd be seeing you again," said Jorms.

Elaine started to walk around him, but he stepped in front of her.

"Let me alone!" she said, forcefully.

"Now, honey, that's no way to treat a friend," said Jorms, jeeringly.

"Lee, we'd better get out of here," said Lefty.

"No big hurry, Lefty. After all, it's not every day a guy gets to see his best girl," said Jorms.

"I'm not your girl and I'm not your friend!" retorted Elaine. "Now, will you get out of my way?"

"Now you've hurt my feelings," said Jorms, reaching out and grabbing her wrist.

Elaine reached out with her other hand and slapped his face, hard. His face contorted with rage. He pulled her to him and attempted to kiss her. She twisted her face away from him and screamed.

Inside Ed Landers's store, Bob Holiday looked up from the seeds he was checking and said, "That sounded like Elaine."

Running out to the street, with Ed on his heels, Bob saw Elaine struggling in the arms of a huge man.

"What do you think you're doing? Let her go!" he yelled.

"Get lost, old man!" snarled Jorms.

Holiday rushed at Jorms, and attempted to grab his arm. A huge fist caught Holiday squarely on the jaw, and he crumpled to the ground, unconscious.

31

Meanwhile, up the street, Lane Streeter had just come out of Gomez Leather Works, when he heard the scream. He was puzzled as to what it was all about when he saw the struggling figures. He hurried down to where the action was. There he saw Elaine trying to free herself from Jorms's grasp.

"Mister, you've just built up some big trouble for yourself!" he yelled. "What do you think you're doing? Let go of that girl, right now!"

By now, quite a crowd had gathered. Jorms looked at Lane and released Elaine. "Now I suppose you're going to be Mr. Hero," he snarled.

"Lane, please, I don't want you having any trouble with him," Elaine pleaded

"You're too late, little girl," said Jorms, grinning. "When fools try to interfere with me, they get what's coming to them."

"Mister Big Mouth, you've been asking for this for a long time, and now you're going to get it," said Lane.

"Sonny boy, I'm going to chew you up and spit you out!" snarled Jorms.

"Stop right where you're at!" a voice roared.

They all looked around to see Sheriff Cantwell coming up on the scene.

"It's all right, Sheriff," said Lane. "This guy doesn't have any manners, so I'm going to teach him some. Come on, big mouth, you're the one doing all the talking."

Beyond himself with rage, Jorms gave a strange growl and leaped at Lane. He threw a vicious left hook that missed as Lane ducked. What happened then was beyond everyone's imagination. A long left hand reached out and gathered the folds of Jorms's shirt and vest. He was lifted off the ground as though he were a child. Lane then shook him the way a big dog would shake a rat. As he lowered Jorms to the ground, he swung his right fist in a whistling arc. It caught Jorms squarely on the jaw and sent him flying off to the side where he collided with the hitch rail. Jorms fell to ground, completely unconscious. It was apparent to all gathered there that his jaw was broken, for it hung all askew.

"I saw it, but I don't believe it!" said Ed Landers. "That just ain't possible, but he did it."

"That man needs a doctor bad," spoke up another.

Lane went to Elaine and took her in his arms. "Are you all right, honey? Did he hurt you?" he asked.

"No, I'm all right but, Lane, I was so frightened. I was afraid he would hurt you," she said, sobbing.

"No, he was all false alarm," Lane said.

The crowd was now dispersing and Lane espied Lefty on the edge of those who remained. "Are you picking this up?" asked Lane.

"I wasn't bothering her," said Lefty. "Ask her if I said anything to her."

"No, he really didn't, Lane," said Elaine. "In fact, he tried to get that other man to leave."

"Okay, friend, but if you ever bother this girl, you had better head for the hills!" said Lane, vehemently.

"You got no call to speak to me like that, and if you ever come after me, you'd better be wearing a gun!" retorted Lefty.

"I'm going to be from now on," said Lane, "and if you're so anxious to die, you're welcome to try."

Doc Baldwin now appeared on the scene, and immediately stooped down and began ministering to Jorms.

"Holy smokes, what happened to him?" Doc asked.

Hi Walker was among those who remained of the crowd. "He was bothering Elaine Holiday and Lane Streeter took him to task for it. Doc, you never saw anybody get hit any harder than this gent. He went down like he was hit by a pole ax or something."

"His jaw is shattered," said Doc. "I could have told him if he wanted trouble, don't pick on Lane Streeter. How many times did he hit him?"

"That's just it, Doc, Lane only hit him once!" said Hi, excitedly. "And before he hit him, he picked him up with one hand and shook him."

"How about some of you boys helping me get him to my office," said Doc. "He's going to be out of commission for some time." It took five men to carry the unconscious Jorms to Doc's office.

Meanwhile, Sheriff Cantwell was talking to Lane and Elaine. "It's just possible that that fellow will be easier to live with now. I must admit, boy, for a while there I was afraid you broke his neck. You know, son, your dad told me once that you were exceptionally strong, but I never dreamed you were that strong."

"I guess I just hit him with a lucky punch," said Lane.

Bob Holiday had long since regained consciousness. "How can I ever thank you, Lane?" he asked. "He knocked me cold with one punch."

"No thanks necessary, Mr. Holiday," said Lane. "I'm just glad I was handy."

"Well, let's get our shopping finished and get home, Elaine. Your mother will be getting worried."

"I'll see you in a few days, honey," said Lane.

10

Doc Baldwin pulled up at the hitch rack at the Redfields' Rocking R Ranch, tied his horse and went to the door. He was there to tend to Tom, who had been taken there to recuperate from the beating he had received from Jorms. John met him at the door.

"Come in, Doc," he said. "Tom's feeling somewhat better, but he still has a way to go."

"If he's smart, he won't try to push it," said Doc. "And I've got some news for you; the guy who did this to him is in worse shape than Tom."

"What do you mean, Doc? Did somebody shoot him?" asked John.

"I'll tell you about it in Tom's room; he'll want to hear it, too," said Doc.

They walked upstairs and into the room where Tom was lying on the bed.

"Hi, Doc," said Tom. "How soon can I get out of this bed?"

"You just take your time about that," said Doc. "It takes time for ribs to heal properly."

"Doc has some news about that guy who did this to you; says he's in worse shape than you," said John.

"How's that, Doc? Did somebody kill him?" asked Tom.

"You guys aren't going to believe this, but it's the truth," said Doc. "Tom, I always thought that you were about the toughest guy around these parts, but see what you make of this. This guy, Jorms, as you well know, is one rough brawler."

"You're telling me!" interjected Tom. "I thought I was

35

run through a meat grinder."

Doc was by now unwrapping the bandages from Tom's body.

"Hmm, starting to look better, but look at those bruises," said Doc.

Tom's body was a mass of discoloration. Huge purple and black bruises covered his body.

"Go on, Doc, you were saying—" said Tom.

"Yes, well, this Jorms was deviling Lane Streeter's girlfriend, Elaine. Well, about that time Lane comes down the street and accosted him about it. From what they tell me, Jorms lets her go with the idea of beating Lane into a pulp. Well, gentlemen, hush! They tell me Lane grabbed him with one hand and lifted him into the air and shook him 'til he rattled. Then when he lowered him to the ground, he really laid one on him. He just hit him with one punch, but what a punch! It took me four hours to set his jaw. It was broken in three places. Result being that Mr. Jorms is going to be laid up for some time. His whole head is one solid bruise," concluded Doc.

"Lane Streeter did that?" asked Tom. "He's just a kid, and he's always seemed so easygoing. I never dreamed he was so tough."

"Well, I've known for some time that he's poison with a gun, but I never knew he was as strong as he is," said Doc. "Now, this is between us, if you don't mind, but one day I was out there to see his sister; she had a cold or something, I don't remember what. Lane didn't know it, but I saw him practicing with a six-gun. Up until then, I always believed that Morg Streeter was the fastest man I had ever seen. Now I don't think Morg could work a gun as fast as Lane."

"You're kidding!" said Tom.

"Gospel truth," said Doc, "so if Friend Jorms has any

ideas of getting even with a gun, he better forget it. Well, Tom, I think you are going to be okay, but just take it easy for at least a week; above all, don't try to get on a horse."

"I'll try, Doc, but I'm not going to promise anything," said Tom, "and thanks for the information."

Doc left and headed back for town.

"Boy, Dad, doesn't that shock you, about Lane and everything that happened?" asked Tom.

"Well, I guess we learn something new every day," his dad answered.

When Doc arrived back in town, he immediately went to the hotel where Jorms was staying until he was sufficiently recovered to travel. Doc walked into the room and found Lefty there with Jorms. "How soon will he be able to get out of here, Doc?" asked Lefty.

"Well, his jaw will take at least two months to heal, so that means those wires will have to stay in place that long," said Doc. "He won't be able to eat right or talk right during that time. Other than that, he probably could leave in about a week. Those bones should be knitted enough by then to get on a horse. Why? Are you in a hurry to get out of here or something?"

"We're supposed to meet some friends of ours in a few days," ventured Lefty.

"If you leave here before a week, don't depend on me to take those wires out; as far as that goes, any doctor could do it," said Doc. "Above all, don't get in another scrap; if you get socked on that jaw again, it could kill you."

He spread some salve on the bruised portions of Jorms's face and head.

"This is very soothing and will reduce the swelling," Doc explained. "Well, be seeing you." He left the room.

Lefty followed him to the door, and when he was satisfied that he was gone, he sat down beside Jorms.

"Lee, this is Wednesday; Brady and the boys will be here on Saturday to do the job. We weren't planning to leave town with them anyway, so you can stay here and we'll meet them back at the hideout later and collect our share," said Lefty. "If I can get that young fool in a shootout, I'll blast him to kingdom come."

Jorms nodded his agreement.

11

Lane and Renny had just finished separating twenty more horses.

"When is Mr. Rowan picking up this bunch, Lane?" asked Renny.

"Friday, about nine o'clock," answered Lane. "He didn't want the broken ones; he has a wrangler there who can break them. He wants to save as much money as he can."

"Boy, Lane, I wish I could have been there the other day when you laid that Jorms out!" exclaimed Renny. "I took Mom to the dining room for dinner with that extra money you gave me, and Aunt Abby says that that Jorms is a sight."

"Renny, it's never pleasant to mix in anything like that," said Lane. "I'm sorry it happened, but sometimes we have to do things that we're sorry for."

"Well, do me a favor, will you? Don't ever get mad at me," said Renny, laughing. "Anything else for today?"

"No, that's it for today," said Lane. "I'll see you tomorrow."

Lane walked over to the house. His mother and Callie were baking some more apple pies.

"Oh, boy, just what I needed," he said, tickling Callie in the ribs.

She screamed and slapped him on the arm, thereby leaving a streak of flour on his sleeve. He laughed and said, "Oh, that's right; Renny wanted me to give you a kiss for him, but I told him to do his own kissing."

"Mom, make him stop that!" she retorted.

"Oh, you mean you want Mom to stop Renny from

kissing you?" he said, grinning.

"That's not what I meant and you know it!" she said.

"Well, Renny will be pleased that you don't want Mom to stop him from kissing you," said Lane.

"Oh, Lane, you're impossible," said Martha, laughing. "But let's talk in a more serious vein."

"Sure, Mom, what's on your mind?" he asked.

"Well, Saturday is shopping day again; I swear I don't know where the time goes. We want to get an early start," she said. "Can you have the buggy hitched up for us?"

"Sure, Mom, and tell you what; I'm selling twenty more horses to Mr. Rowan, and to show you there's no hard feelings for Callie slapping me, I'll treat you all to dinner again," Lane said, and then added innocently, "and Callie can even invite Renny."

"Lord, give me strength!" exclaimed Callie.

"That will be nice, Lane," said Martha. "Would you want to ask the Holidays if they could join us? I'm going over there tomorrow."

"Oh, let him go, Mom, that way he can get to see Miss Wonderful again," said Callie.

"You do get some good ideas now and then, Callie, but Renny and I are going to be busy all day tomorrow, so I guess Mom can invite them," said Lane.

The next day Lane and Renny spent inspecting many of the horses for cuts and bruises that they might have incurred. They found several of them and Lane doctored them up.

"Bruises usually aren't so bad, but cuts can get infected if they aren't taken care of," said Lane. "Before you started working here, I had to shoot a horse because he was so badly infected. He would have died anyway, his leg was so swollen. I'd rather put them out of their misery when they are like that."

The day was far spent by the time they had finished, so Renny took off for home.

"Be here about seven, Renny. That will give us plenty of time to have these horses ready for Cal," said Lane.

*   *   *

It was precisely nine o'clock when Cal Rowan, along with three of his hands, pulled up at the corral.

"Hi, there, Lane. All ready for us, I see," said Cal. He was the owner of the C-R Connected ranch, southeast of Haleyville. "Yeah, we're all set; twenty horses, as ordered," said Lane.

"Lane, what's this I hear about you having some trouble in town the other day?" asked Gil Robertson, Cal's foreman.

"Oh, nothing much," replied Lane.

"That's not what we heard," said Cal. "How badly was that guy hurt, anyway?"

"I don't think he's too serious," said Lane.

"Oh, no, Lane just broke his jaw!" exclaimed Renny.

"Well, the next time a grizzly gets after my stock, I'll just get you to wrestle with him," said Cal, grinning. "Well, here's your money, Lane."

He handed Lane a check and added, "C'mon, boys, let's get these critters home."

"Thank you, Mr. Rowan," said Lane. "Be seeing you around."

12

"Okay, Lefty, you got us all together for a reason. Now, what is so important that we should know?" asked Brady Hatch. He, along with Hank, Bill, and Boley had gathered at the hideout in response to Lefty's summons.

"Some things have happened since we talked last, and I just thought you should know about them," answered Lefty.

"What kind of things?" asked Brady.

"Lee Jorms got the beating of his life the other day, and—,"

"You mean Tom Redfield whipped him?" interrupted Brady.

"No, let me finish," said Lefty. "That kid, Lane Streeter, who you said was only nineteen and wouldn't be a bother to us, knocked the living daylights out of Jorms. His jaw is broke in three places, and, in short, he's a mess. Now, I can still set that building on fire and all that, but, what I want to know is, do you still want to go through with it?"

"What about Tom Redfield? Did Jorms put him out of commission?" asked Bill.

"Yeah, Lee gave him a bad enough beating that he won't be getting around for several weeks," said Lefty. "Lee was feeling his oats about that and was bothering a girl in town, and this Lane Streeter got on him about it. You won't believe this, but Streeter hit him with only one punch."

"That is hard to believe," said Hank. "I didn't think anyone could whip Jorms."

"Well, what about it, boys, do you still want to go

through with it?" asked Lefty.

"How good is this kid with a gun?" asked Brady. "Just because he's good with his fists doesn't mean he can use a gun."

"I don't know, I've never seen him use a gun," said Lefty. "But I told him if he ever comes after me, he'd better be wearing a gun. I think I could take him, if it comes down to that."

"Well, I'm all for going on with our plans, but it's up to you boys. What do you think about it?" asked Brady.

"Okay with me," said Hank. "We can always shoot that kid if we have to."

"Same here," said Bill. "He's only one man."

"How about you, Boley, are you in?" asked Brady.

"Yeah, you can count me in. But I'll tell you the truth, I don't like killing anybody," said Boley.

"I don't either," said Brady. "Lefty, any chance you could put him out of the way by Saturday?"

"I'll try it," said Lefty. "But I'm not promising anything. He doesn't come into town that often, and the holdup is only two days away."

"Okay, we go on as planned," said Brady. "Any further questions?" Hearing none, he said, "See you Saturday, boys."

13

Morg and Martha Streeter had always been family oriented, and when Lane was a little child, his dad would sometimes allow him to go to the office with him. Morg had made Lane a little wooden gun, and ofttimes when Morg was out patrolling the town or out on a case, Lane would play his childish games. One of his favorite games was to look at the wanted posters, which his father had quite a few of, and pretend that he had met the men face to face. Some of them were famous names like Web Stocker, Billy the Kid, Brady Hatch, and quite a few others. Lane would pore over the wanted posters and try to memorize all their features.

"All right, Stocker, cut lose your wolf or leave town before sundown!" Lane would challenge the outlaw. Usually, in his imagination, the bad man would draw and he would be forced to kill him. What he didn't realize was how many of these faces he remembered, and that even though the games were past history, he could still remember some of their features, and what they were wanted for. For instance, Stocker was a noted gunman, while Hatch was a bank robber, and Wyatt Earp was a famous marshal, like his dad. He wasn't thinking of these things now, as he, his mother and sister were on their way to town on this Saturday morning.

"We sure needed that rain we got last night," his mother remarked.

"I'll say," said Lane, "and what I like is how cool it is."

They pulled into town around nine o'clock and he pulled up in front of Ed Landers's store.

"I'll be in Mr. Gomez's shop and then I'm going to the

bank to cash this check," he said, and then added, "I had hoped to deposit most of it, but if I'm buying Callie's dinner, I'll need it."

Callie made a face at him and grinned. As Lane got out of the buggy, he noticed two strange riders coming into town. He nodded to them, got a nod in return and started up the street. All of a sudden, he felt as if he should know one of the men. He tried to remember where he might have seen him, but it just wouldn't register. "Must be my imagination," he muttered to himself. He started to walk farther when it suddenly struck him.

"That one rider was Brady Hatch!" he exclaimed to himself. "What's he doing here?"

Lane changed direction and, instead, headed for the sheriff's office. He went inside expecting to find Sheriff Cantwell seated at his desk. But Rufus Harms, an old-timer who worked around the office, was seated there.

"Is the sheriff here, Rufe?" Lane asked.

"Nope," said Rufe. "He got notice that Cal Rowan wanted to see him about some stolen horses. Some strangers rode in and told him."

"How long ago was this?" asked Lane.

"About a half hour ago," said Rufe. "There were two of them."

"Did you ever see either of them before?" asked Lane.

"No, I can't say as I did," said Rufe.

"Rufe, do you mind if I go through some of these wanted posters?" asked Lane. "I'm curious about something."

"Go to it, Lane," said Rufe. "Here, sit down here."

Lane seated himself and got some wanted posters out of the drawer. As he went through them, he tried to remember how long ago he had seen the poster with

Brady Hatch's picture on it. He went through quite a few of them until he came to the one he wanted.

"I wasn't sure this one was still here," he commented.

"Somebody you know?" asked Rufe.

"I'm not sure," said Lane, "but I think so. Thanks, Rufe, see you later."

Leaving the jail, Lane headed straight for the bank. Blaine Hallowell had been the owner of the bank as long as Lane could remember.

"Is Mr. Hallowell in, Angie?" he asked the girl at the receptionist's desk.

"Yes, I'll tell him you are here, Lane," answered Angie. She went into an office and reappeared immediately.

"Go right in, Lane," she said.

"Thank you, Angie." He smiled, and walked into Mr. Hallowell's office.

"Hi, Lane, what can I do for you?" asked Mr. Hallowell. "Say, what's with the gun? I don't ever remember seeing you wearing one before."

"Just a precaution," said Lane. "Mr. Hallowell, I want to talk to you about something; maybe it's nothing, but I want to see what you think about it."

"All right, go ahead, Lane," said Mr. Hallowell. "I don't think I've ever seen you looking this serious before."

"This could be serious business. Mr. Hallowell, have you ever heard of Brady Hatch?" asked Lane.

"You mean Brady Hatch, the bank robber? Who hasn't heard of him? Why? What's he got to do with this?" asked Mr. Hallowell.

"Let's go back a ways," said Lane. "Not bragging about my dad, you understand, but after he became sheriff, this town became pretty tame."

"You can say that again," said Mr. Hallowell. "Lane,

46

he did such a good job that all outlaws steered clear of Haleyville."

"Well, Dad's dead now, and not taking anything away from Mr. Cantwell, but he doesn't have Dad's reputation. Now, see what you think of this: Brady Hatch is in town along with three other strangers," said Lane.

"Well, couldn't that be a coincidence?" asked Mr. Hallowell.

"Put this together with that fact and you tell me if you think it's a coincidence," said Lane. "Who do you think is the toughest guy around these parts?"

"Until the other day, I would have said Tom Redfield. Now, I'm not so sure," Mr. Hallowell smiled. "From what I hear, you kind of took the wind out of that fellow's sails."

Lane's face reddened. "Mr. Hallowell, that Jorms deliberately picked that fight with Tom. Why? Tom admits that he had never seen Jorms before. Now, just supposing you were planning to hold up the bank or something? Wouldn't you try to make it as safe as possible?"

"Yes-s-s, I suppose I would. What are you getting at?" asked Mr. Hallowell.

"Just this," said Lane. "First, Tom is put out of commission; Brady Hatch is in town; Sheriff Cantwell is called out of town about a so-called case of stolen horses and—"

"Why do you say 'so-called' case?" asked Mr. Hallowell.

"One of those strangers brought him the word," said Lane. "To me, there are too many coincidences to be just that."

"Lane, I agree with you. We had better start taking some precautions," said Mr. Hallowell.

"I'll go round up Gil Evans and Lafe Budrow," said Lane. "Could you—"

"What good could Gil Evans do?" asked Mr. Hallowell.

"I once heard my dad tell my mom that if he was in a tight spot, Gil Evans would be one of the people he could depend on; he's not only a gunsmith, he also served in the Union Army, and Dad said he was a crack shot," said Lane.

"That's good enough for me," said Mr. Hallowell. "And we all know that Lafe is not only a good blacksmith, but he also served with the Rebel Army. You know, Hi Walker is also an ex-army man; I'll see if I can recruit him."

They both left the bank. Lane hurried over to Gil Evans's gunshop.

"Hello, Lane," said Gil. "What can I do for you?"

"I hope nothing," said Lane. "Gil, Mr. Hallowell and I think there's going to be an attempt to hold up the bank, and we have to hurry."

"'Nough said!" answered Gil. He grabbed a gun and followed Lane out of the shop.

As they hurried over to the blacksmith shop, they heard a yell, "Fire, fire!" "Oh, no! It's started already!" exclaimed Lane.

Blaine Hallowell, followed by Hi Walker and Lafe Budrow, came running along the street toward the bank. Each of them was carrying a gun.

As they neared the bank, they saw four horses standing in front of the bank, with a man dressed in blue holding them.

"All right, mister," said Lane. "This is as far as you're going."

The man whirled to face Lane and the others. His hand dropped to the gun at his waist. As the gun was coming to bear, Lane's hand was a blur and flame shot from his gun muzzle; the man howled and dropped his gun. A neat, little hole appeared in his wrist and was now welling blood.

"I give up!" he yelled.

"All right, back over there out of the way and you won't get hurt any more than you are!" said Lane. "Kick that gun over here so you won't be tempted to get foolish."

The man did as he was told and asked, "Is it okay if I tie a 'kerchief around this wrist? It's bleeding all over me."

"Okay, but no funny stuff," warned Lane. "Hi, you're the most experienced with horses; how about you taking those horses down the street a ways?"

Most of the people were unaware of the holdup; they were hurrying to the fire. Just as Hi had led the horses away, the bank door burst open and three men came out with guns in their hands; the leader was holding a large bag in his hand.

"Far enough, Brady!" yelled Lane. "Either drop the guns and the money or all of you are going to die!"

One of the other men raised his gun toward Lane. Gil Evans's gun spoke and the man lurched backward and grabbed his shoulder. His gun dropped to the ground.

"Any more of that and the next one gets it dead center!" yelled Gil.

The other two men dropped their guns and raised their hands.

"And who might you be?" asked Brady, looking at Lane.

"I don't know as it matters, but I'm Lane Streeter," said Lane.

"He was the one who was too young to cause us any

trouble!" snorted the other outlaw.

"You're right, Hank, I was never more wrong," admitted Brady.

"A lot of good that does us now!" snorted Hank. "Well, what comes next?"

"One thing, was anybody hurt in the bank?" asked Lane.

"No, sir, fella!" said Brady. "We're not killers. I don't allow shooting in any holdups I pull."

"Well, Mr. Hallowell, this becomes your show now," said Lane.

"First, somebody go for Doc Baldwin to tend to these men who were shot; next, let's get these other men in jail," said Mr. Hallowell.

People began streaming back from the direction of the fire. Many of them wanted to know what was going on. "What was burning?" asked Lane.

"Just that old abandoned house on the edge of town," spoke up Ed Landers, who had gone to see if there was any danger to the town. "We don't know how it started."

"I think we have a good idea," said Lane.

"You mean you know who started it?" asked Mr. Hallowell.

"I've got a pretty good idea of who it was. Of course, I can't prove it," said Lane. "But I've got a funny feeling it will all come out in the wash."

"We may as well take these two wounded men to Doc's office," said Gil Evans. "That's where he'll want to treat them."

Several men escorted the two to Doc's office, while Lane, Mr. Hallowell, and others took the other outlaws to jail.

14

Later in the day, Lane met his mother and Callie at the dining room. Shortly after they were seated, the Holidays came in and joined them.

"What's this I hear about a bank holdup?" asked Bob Holiday.

Lane explained all that had happened, and added, "I wonder where that Lefty fits into all this."

"Why do you think he had anything to do with it?" asked Martha.

"I can't prove it," said Lane, "but I think he started that fire."

"Will they put him in jail?" asked Callie.

"No, Callie, they have to have proof that he was involved," explained Lane. "And you know he's not going to admit it."

Just then Abby came over to take their order.

"Boy, you don't know how glad I am that you weren't hurt out there!" she exclaimed.

"Thank you, Aunt Abby," Lane smiled. "I'm kind of glad myself."

"It scares me to see you wearing that gun, Lane," said Elaine. "What is this town coming to, anyway?"

"By the way, Aunt Abby, was that man Jorms out of his room at all?" asked Lane.

"No, I don't think so; he is still a pretty sick man, Doc Baldwin says," answered Abby.

"Somehow, I believe he and Lefty are tied in with this whole thing," said Lane. "I don't believe we've heard the last from them yet."

"Oh, don't say that!" exclaimed Elaine. "The whole

thing scares me to death!"

"Well, honey, these things happen, and we have to make the best of them and make sure that the right thing is done," said Lane.

"Truer words were never spoken," said Abby. "And now let me get your orders before this young scamp starts running on me again."

Everyone there knew that she was just trying to put things on a more pleasant plane, so as to remove the pressure. Lane tried to do his part

"What's your special, fried skunk again?" he asked, grinning.

"Elaine, you better get him straightened out before you get married!" said Abby. "Else he'll just find fault with your cooking."

Elaine reddened considerably. "Please, Aunt Abby, don't rush me on something that important!"

Their orders were taken and the meal went on in a more pleasant atmosphere. Abby came in again at the end of their meal.

"Anyone for dessert?" she asked.

"Not me," said Lane, "I'm poisoned enough already."

"Boy, you two!" said Bob. "Abby, I've got to admit that that was an excellent meal."

"There, Mr. Smarty, I guess that will put you in your place!" said Abby, making a snoot at Lane.

He grinned. "The only reason he's saying that is that he knows what a temper you've got."

They all laughed as they walked out together. "Thank you for that fine meal, Martha," said Bob.

"Don't thank me; Lane paid for it," said Martha, laughing. "Of course, we know why he did it. Don't we, Elaine?"

"I thought you were on my side!" she exclaimed.

"I'm on your side, Elaine," said Callie. "We have to stick together against him."

"Mr. Holiday, I can see we're outnumbered; we'd better quit," said Lane.

"You're right, Lane, and thank you again. Well, Jennie, we'd better be getting along home," said Bob. "So long, folks, we'll be seeing you."

15

Renny and Lane were gentling some horses when Sheriff Cantwell came riding in. He dismounted stiffly, and limped over to the corral fence, where he seated himself on the top rail.

"Lane, I'm getting old; all that riding yesterday and now today again. It feels better just to sit down," he groaned.

"What did you find out when you got to Cal's ranch?" asked Lane.

"He wanted to know why I came out; he had never sent for me," said Sheriff Cantwell.

"Just as I thought," said Lane. "Mr. Cantwell, I think that there were six men in on it, not just four."

"That's what I think, too. I wish there was some way we could get Lefty or Jorms to talk," said Sheriff Cantwell.

"Hatch and the others are still in jail?" queried Lane.

"Yes, Judge Warren will be back next week, and then they will have a trial," said the sheriff.

"How long do you think they'll get?" asked Lane.

"Son, I have no idea. Hatch has served time before, so I imagine he'll be put away for a good stretch," said Sheriff Cantwell. "You know, Lane, I kind of like that fellow; he makes no fuss about what happened and he admits he did wrong."

"What about the two who were shot? Are they still at Doc's, or did he say they were okay to put in jail?" asked Lane.

"They're in jail, along with the other two," said the sheriff. "Lane, I want to thank you for what you did. You remind me of your dad all over again."

"That's not for me," said Lane. "I like it peaceful. By the way, Sheriff, have you seen Lefty or Jorms today?"

"I saw Jorms; he's still in his room, but nary hide nor hair of Lefty," said Sheriff Cantwell. "Lane, don't be surprised if I have some news for you that will knock your eyes out."

"What's that, Sheriff?" asked Lane.

"I don't want to say before I'm absolutely sure; maybe it's nothing, but I'll know shortly," said the sheriff.

"Now you really have me curious," said Lane.

"Well, I'll let you know; I've got to be running along. Renny, don't ever get old, it's too hard on you," said the sheriff, smiling. "And don't let this slave driver work you to death."

"Okay, Mr. Cantwell, I'll be careful," said Renny, glad to be included in the conversation.

The sheriff rode off toward town. Renny and Lane started working the horses again and Renny suddenly asked, "Lane, what do you think he meant when he said he might have some news for you?"

"Boy, I wish I knew. I have to admit, he's got me curious," said Lane. "You know, Renny, Sheriff Cantwell is a very shrewd man. He keeps his eyes open even though he doesn't say much."

They finished their work and Renny took off for home. Lane went into the house.

"Lane, wasn't that Sheriff Cantwell?" asked Martha.

"Yes, he came out to thank me for yesterday, but he said something that has me curious," said Lane.

"What was that?" asked Martha.

"We were talking about what happened in town, and he suddenly said that he might have some news that would knock my eyes out," said Lane.

"That is strange," said Martha. "What could he possibly mean?"

"I wish I knew," said Lane. "Oh, well, he said he would let us know shortly. Until then, I guess we'll have to wait."

"I suppose so," she replied. "Son, there's something else; it bothers me to see you wearing a gun. It brings back too many memories. "

"Well, Mom, I think it's necessary right now; as soon as this present trouble dies down, I won't be wearing it anymore," Lane said. "Besides, just think of what could have happened the other day if I hadn't been wearing it."

"That's true, I know, but it still scares me," Martha said.

16

Lefty Bowens rode into town from the west, tied up, and began heading for the dining room when Sheriff Cantwell hailed him. Lefty walked over to him and asked, "Something on your mind, Sheriff?"

"I'm just wondering where you were the other day when the bank was held up," said the sheriff.

"I've been gone for a few days, Sheriff," said Lefty. "Why, was there something you wanted to see me about? You say the bank was held up? When did this happen?"

"Last Saturday," replied the sheriff. "Listen, come over to the office for a few minutes, will you? There's some men I want you to meet, and I would like to ask you a few questions."

"Sure, Sheriff, anything to oblige," answered Lefty, "but I can't think of anything you would want to ask me about."

Lefty, leading his horse, followed the sheriff over to his office.

"You can tie him up there in the shade," said the sheriff, pointing to a spot at the side of the jail. "That's why Morg had that hitch rack built there, so his horse would be in the shade."

"Good idea," said Lefty, as he followed Sheriff Cantwell into the jail.

"Come on in back where the cells are; I want to see if you know any of these men," said the sheriff.

The two men walked to the back of the jail where the cells were, six in all. Two men were in each of the first two cells, two with bandages. Hatch and Boley were in the first cell, and Bill and Hank in the one adjacent to it. The sheriff watched closely to see if there was any sign of recognition in any of the men.

"Who's that, a new deputy?" asked Hatch.

"Have any of you men ever seen this man before?" asked Sheriff Cantwell.

"Not me," said Hatch. "How about you boys?"

They all replied in the negative, so the sheriff beckoned Lefty back to the office.

"Lefty, you sure have a nice horse there," commented the sheriff. "He's got a few years on him, but he still looks sound. How long have you had him?"

Lefty, warming up to this friendly attitude of the sheriff, said, "Yeah, he's a good horse all right. He's around twelve; I got him when he was just a colt. He's not for sale, if that's what you have in mind."

"Well, it never does any harm to ask. Thanks, Lefty, you've been very cooperative," said the sheriff.

"Any time, Sheriff," said Lefty. As he walked out, he had a puzzled look on his face.

As soon as the sheriff saw Lefty mount his horse and take off down the street, he hurried down the street the other direction. He walked into a small shop that had a sign above it reading "Garcia Pottery Works." A small man, obviously of Mexican descent, came to meet him.

"Ah, Sheriff Cantwell, what can I do for you?" he asked.

"Pedro, do you remember about ten years ago I had you make a cast of a horse's hoof?" asked the sheriff.

"Sí, sí, Sheriff; eet was out at Bernadillo Springs when Señor Streeter was keeled," replied Garcia.

"Do you think you could make another one for me? It is right up by my office," said Sheriff Cantwell.

"Oh, but certainly, Señor Sheriff," replied Garcia. "I weel get my stuff ready and be right up."

"Thank you, Pedro," said the sheriff. "Oh, by the way, if anybody sees you doing it, kind of cut off working until they leave. I would rather that nobody knows about this, just like before."

"That's the way eet weel be," said Pedro.

Sheriff Cantwell waited until Pedro had everything he needed, and they walked to the sheriffs office. The sheriff took Pedro around to the side where the hitch rail was.

"I wet this ground down real good so the tracks would be easier to get," said the sheriff.

"Thees ees good," said Pedro. "But first I must let eet dry."

"Sure, you know your business better than I do, Pedro," the sheriff said. "I'll be over in the dining room if you need me. Just put the cast in the office like the last time. And thanks again."

"But, of course," said Pedro, smiling.

17

Judge Alec Warren arrived back in Haleyville eight days after the attempted holdup. Meeting him at the stage, Sheriff Cantwell had apprised him of the events of the past week. Judge Warren was a man in his late sixties, but he was still very active and was possessed of a keen mind. He had been appointed to the office of judge by the governor many years before. He was very strict, but also very fair. Thus it was, when on the following Monday morning, court was in session.

The courtroom was crowded, as everyone in town was interested in what was going on. All those who were involved in the case had been asked by Sheriff Cantwell to be there. Lane Streeter, along with his mother and Callie, were seated in the front row. The defendants were seated off to the side, along with the sheriff. They were all handcuffed. Most of these proceedings were rather informal, so the judge opened the proceedings.

"All right, Sheriff Cantwell, what do we have here this morning?" he asked.

"Your Honor, we have these four men who tried to hold up the bank on April 29th, last Saturday," replied the sheriff.

"What are their names?" asked the judge.

"Brady Hatch, William Leathers, Henry Baker, and Boland West," replied Sheriff Cantwell.

"Are you men represented by an attorney?" asked the judge.

"Nope, we don't need one, Judge," answered Brady. "We done it, so why waste time on all that legal hullabaloo?"

"Brady, how many times have you been up before a judge on this same charge?" asked Judge Warren, with a smile on his face.

"I done lost count, Judge," said Brady.

The courtroom exploded with laughter, among with Judge Warren.

"Won't you ever learn?" asked the judge.

"Well, Judge, a man has to make a living," responded Brady.

Once again, laughter broke out. Asking for order, Judge Warren continued.

"Sheriff, was there anybody hurt in the holdup?" asked the judge.

"Only two of the prisoners, Judge," answered Sheriff Cantwell. "You can see their bandages."

"Yes, I see," said the judge. "Is there anything else about this case that should be considered at this time?"

Just as Lane Streeter rose to his feet, two men came in the open door of the courtroom. They were Lefty Bowens and Lee Jorms. Jorms's face was still horribly swollen and bruised. He glared around the room, as though daring anyone to make a comment about his face.

"You have something to offer, young man?" the judge asked.

"Yes, I—"

"State your name, young man," remonstrated the judge.

"I'm sorry, Your Honor, my name is Lane Streeter," said Lane.

"By any chance, are you related to Morgan Streeter?" asked the judge, knowing full well that he was.

"He was my father," answered Lane.

"Very well, proceed with what you have to offer," said Judge Warren.

"It seemed apparent to Sheriff Cantwell and me that there were at least two more accomplices in the holdup," said Lane. "It's true that we can't at this time prove it."

"If you don't have enough proof to offer, young man, you had better not accuse anybody of anything, or you could really get yourself in trouble," said Judge Warren,

"All right, Judge," said Lane. "Then I have nothing further to offer."

"Does anyone else have anything else to offer about this case?" asked the judge. "This is highly irregular, but, if these men are willing to plead guilty, and are ready to be sentenced, then I see no reason why we can't clear this up right away."

"We're ready, Judge," said Brady. "We done talked this over and we figger we're as ready as we'll ever be."

"Sheriff, will you please escort these men to the front of the court?" asked the judge.

The sheriff followed the men to the bench where they lined up before the judge.

"Brady, how many years did you get the last time you were sentenced?" asked Judge Warren.

"Ten years, Judge, but I only served three of those years," said Brady. "I got out early for good behavior."

"All right, can you vouch for these other men?" asked the judge.

"What do you mean, Judge?" asked Brady. "Do you mean will they listen to me?"

"Just this," said Judge Warren, "I'm willing to give you boys a break if you will do as I tell you."

"That sounds good to me, Judge," said Brady. "What do you have in mind?"

"Brady, I've heard a lot about you down through the years, and not much of it good," said Judge Warren. "But

I've also heard that once you make a promise, you never break it. Is that true?"

"Only once I broke a promise, Judge," said Brady, "and I really couldn't help that."

"How was that, Brady?" asked the judge.

Brady smiled. "Once I promised a sheriff that I would meet him at a certain place, and I couldn't be there."

"Why was that?" asked the judge.

"I was in jail," smiled Brady.

Once again the courtroom erupted in laughter.

"All right, here's my proposition, boys; it's up to you," the judge stated. "If you boys will promise that you will never show your face in this town again, I will sentence you to five years each, with the provision that you can get out early with good behavior. How does that sound?"

All the men smiled and nodded. "That sounds great to me, Judge," said Boley. "I'll make that promise."

"How about the rest of you boys? Does that sound all right to you?" asked the judge.

"That's more than fair, Judge," said Brady. "We'll do it."

"Sheriff, I'll leave it up to you to see that these men are taken to the State Prison," said Judge Warren. "I'll have the necessary papers on your desk in the morning."

The sheriff went to the front of the courtroom, and he and the judge conversed in low tones. He then went back to his prisoners and prepared to escort them to jail.

"We will ask everyone in the courtroom to remain seated until the sheriff gets back," announced the judge. "He has another matter to bring to our attention."

Immediately there went up all kinds of whisperings as to what the sheriff might be bringing before them.

Martha asked Lane if this was something he knew

anything about. He assured her he didn't know anything about it, and told her that he was as curious as she. Several people got up, stretched and sat down again.

"Judge, is it okay if we leave?" asked Lefty. "We're really not part of the town, so anything the sheriff brings up can't be of any interest to us."

"We would rather you stayed," said the judge. "He said he would be right back."

Just then Sheriff Cantwell walked back into the courtroom. A hush fell over those assembled there, in expectation of what was to come.

"Judge, I hope you will bear with me in what I am about to do," began the sheriff, "but this is very important."

"I hardly know where to begin," continued the sheriff, "so I'll just review some happenings of the past. When Morg Streeter was killed about nine years ago, most of you know that I was his deputy. That case has been with me ever since, and recently some new evidence has come up. At the time of his death, I went out to the scene of the crime. I have never told anyone what I found, hoping that something would come forth to add to what I already have. Well, in the last few weeks, that something did appear."

By now everybody in the courtroom was all attention. Lane Streeter leaned forward, as though by doing so, he would miss nothing of what was being said.

The sheriff went on. "First of all, I will acquaint you with what I found the first time I went out there. Morg was evidently on his way home, as the tracks showed, coming from the south. He met a man coming from the north, as the tracks again showed. This man was the killer. They had a brief conversation, and the man rode on. Morg stopped at Bernadillo Springs and had knelt down to get a drink. There had been a good rain the day before, so the tracks were plain.

"Meanwhile, this other man had gone on a ways, and then stopped, dismounted, walked back on foot and hid behind a small clump of alders that was there. Seeing Morg kneeling, and not suspecting anything, the killer then shot Morg in the back, the bullet going on through his heart. The killer then went back for his horse, and this is where he made his mistake. He rode back to the spring, dismounted and knelt over Morg to make certain he was dead. When he knelt down, he knelt on his left knee as a left-handed man would do. His right boot print was right beside the imprint of his knee."

By this time, a new appreciation for the abilities of Sheriff Josh Cantwell was in the minds of the people in the room. Many of them had thought that he was a man who just went about the job of being a sheriff, with no great aptitude for the job. He now had their undivided attention.

The sheriff went on: "The killer's horse walked on over to the spring to get a drink. In doing so, his hoof prints were very plain. His left front hoof was very irregular; in fact, you might say, deformed. The hoof toed in to the right. The horse also rubbed himself on the wooden framework that was built there."

The sheriff now took an envelope from his pocket and opened it. From it, he extracted several hairs.

"These hairs were taken from that horse," he said. "I had Pedro Garcia go out there and take a plaster cast of that one hoof. As you all know, Pedro is a master at what he does. He first poured plaster into the print and allowed it to dry. After it was good and dry, he then put a fine glaze on it so the new plaster wouldn't adhere to it. He then poured a new batch of plaster into a container and placed the first cast into the new batch. This made a perfect print, which I now show you."

He held up a box and withdrew an object that was wrapped in cloth. He had another object in another box.

"Folks, you might think I'm running on considerable, but just bear with me," he said.

"Sheriff, you just go on and take all the time you want," spoke up Judge Warren. "This gets more interesting by the minute."

"Thank you, Judge," he said. "Well, let's go back again a few more years. I think it was about fifteen years ago, I'm not real sure, but Morg Streeter told me that when he was a young fellow, he once had a run-in with a man you have all heard about, the gunfighter, Web Stocker. Now, Web was right-handed and Morg knew this. Not wanting to kill him, Morg simply shot him in the right hand. Stocker disappeared from sight about that time.

"Now, this is speculation on my part, but it's my belief that Stocker was practicing with his left hand until he became just as good as he had been with his right. I further believe that all through those years he had built up a hatred for Morg Streeter. Now, you are all wondering what that has to do with us here today. About a month or so ago, a man came riding into town on a horse that fits the description of the first horse I've been telling you about. I had Pedro Garcia take a similar cast as he had done before. Pedro, what did you find?"

Pedro Garcia rose to his feet. "Señor Sheriff, I swear thees ees the same horse; the shoe ees somewhat deeferent, but I theenk eet ees the same horse."

The sheriff picked up on his comments again. "That man is in this courtroom now and—no, Lefty, you're not going anywhere; you've been covered since you came in."

"That's right, Lefty," broke in a new voice. "Gil Evans here, and I've had a rifle on you since you first walked in."

Lefty Bowens had risen to his feet. "You punk sheriff, you're just trying to railroad me!" he snarled. "That was all guesswork and you know it!"

Sheriff Cantwell held up his hand for silence. "To further prove what I've told you, I asked Lefty how long he's had that gray he rides; he told me that horse is about twelve years old. It's a favorite of his and now it's going to send him to a hangman's rope. Lefty, hold up your right hand and spread your fingers."

Lefty reluctantly did so; the hand was noticeably warped and there was a small indentation as from a bullet hole.

"I guess you know by now that this is really Web Stocker," said Sheriff Cantwell.

The crowd gasped. Martha Streeter exclaimed, "Well, I never!"

Judge Warren took control once more. "Lefty, or whatever your name is, do you have anything to say?"

"All right, all right, so I'm Web Stocker. And you're right, Sheriff, I've hated Morg Streeter's guts for all these years! You don't know what it's like, feeling helpless while learning to use your other hand. When I got the chance, I gunned him, and I'm glad of it!" snarled Lefty.

Pandemonium now reigned in the courtroom. Everybody wanted to talk at once. Lee Jorms had also risen, and he now glared around the room.

"Everybody sit down and be quiet! Let's have order!" yelled Judge Warren. It was several minutes before quiet was restored.

"Now, I want everyone to be quiet so we can get on with the proceedings," said the judge. "Lefty, I have a question for you; were you in on the attempted holdup?"

"You'll never know, Judge!" he snarled.

"You might as well tell us, Stocker," said the sheriff. "It won't make any difference to you anyway."

Lane Streeter now stood to his feet. "May I say something, Judge?" he asked.

"Certainly," said Judge Warren.

Lane turned to face Jorms. "Why did you beat up on Tom Redfield, Jorms?" he asked.

Jorms' jaw was still tightly wired shut, so it was hard for him to speak, but he managed to mutter, "He started the fight."

"That won't do, Jorms; too many witnesses saw the fight, and they all agree that you purposely picked that fight," broke in the sheriff. "You might as well tell us why."

Jorms just shook his head and started to leave the courtroom. Martha started to say something, but was restrained by Lane.

"The sheriff can't hold him, Mom, he has no evidence to hold him on."

"Sheriff, I want you to arrest Stocker and hold him for trial," directed Judge Warren. "He will be held for murder. Stocker, your trial will be held at a later date."

Sheriff Cantwell walked back to Stocker and disarmed him. "Well, I have to admit, Stocker, you had me fooled; I never dreamed you were Web Stocker. You sure have changed your appearance."

With the trial over, the courtroom quickly cleared. John Redfield, who had been in attendance with his sons, came over to Lane. "Lane, Martha, you'll never know how happy I am that this has been cleared up about Morg. I'm sure this has bothered you these many years, not knowing. Well, for my money, Josh Cantwell is a lot of sheriff."

"Thank you, John," said Martha. "Yes, you are right, it has bothered me. I thought it would be one of those crimes that would never be solved."

"I think it's amazing the way Sheriff Cantwell worked this whole thing out," said Lane. "And to think, he had all that evidence for years and never told anyone; he certainly had more patience than I would have had."

When the Streeters got home that evening, Martha sat down at the kitchen table, put her face in her arms, and softly cried. Lane and Callie got on either side of her and tried to console her.

"Mom, for your sake, I'm glad this is finally settled; maybe now we can get on with our lives," said Lane.

"There's still the trial, and that won't be easy," said Martha.

18

Lane was busy putting the finishing touches on a big bay that Tom Redfield had seen in the holding corral and was interested in. He had taken special pains with this particular horse, for he wanted Tom to be pleased with it. The horse was as ready now as it would ever be, and Lane was happy with the results. Just as he was unsaddling the big horse, he heard a voice excitedly calling him. He looked up the lane that led to the main pasture where he kept the horses that were completely broken and gentled for riding stock. He had sent Renny to bring three horses that he had a possible sale for. Now, Renny was galloping his horse at a fast pace.

"Lane, Lane!" he yelled. "Come quick!"

"What's wrong, Renny?" Lane asked.

"There are three strange horses in the pasture!" he said. "That Appaloosa is gone and probably two others."

Lane quickly saddled Midnight, and he and Renny hurried to the pasture. Renny pointed out the three horses that he had noticed. The brands read Circle T.

"Whoever left these broncs here probably traded for some reason," said Lane. "Sometimes a sheriff will do that when the posse he's leading needs new horses."

"Is he allowed to do that?" asked Renny.

"The problem with that is that we don't have a bill of sale for these broncs," explained Lane. "If these guys are crooked, they could come back later and claim these horses and say they were stolen from them."

"Gee, Lane, what should we do?" asked Renny.

"Let's see if we can find out which way they headed when they left here," said Lane.

They went back to the pasture gate and, after a little while, Lane found tracks.

"They seem to be headed toward town," he announced. "Renny, go back to the barn and bring back three hackamores. We'll take these horses to town and see if we can find the ones they took. I'd sure hate to lose that big Appaloosa."

While Renny went for the hackamores, Lane checked the horses over. They seemed to be in good condition, except that they were slightly jaded, probably from hard running. When Renny returned, they put the hackamores on the three horses and started for town. When they got as far as the house, Lane went in and buckled on his gunbelt.

"Do you think they'll give us trouble?" asked Renny, his eyes wide.

"I hope not," said Lane, "but we won't take any chances."

When they got to town, Lane decided to inform Sheriff Cantwell of what had happened. As they were passing the Lone Eagle Saloon, they saw the three horses that were missing, with the familiar Slash S brand on their hips.

"C'mon, Renny, let's change these saddles onto their own broncs," said Lane. "After that, we'll ask some questions."

As Lane and Renny were switching the saddles, Lane heard a voice calling him. Sheriff Cantwell had just come out of the hotel dining room and was crossing the street.

"I saw those horses with your brand and I figgered you had made another sale," he said.

"No, Renny found these three Circle T broncs in the pasture this morning, and we found that whoever left them switched horses on me," said Lane. "Now, it may be perfectly on the level, but I'm wondering why they didn't come to the house and tell me about it."

"Let's find out," said the sheriff.

"Renny, you stay here and watch the horses," said Lane.

Lane and the sheriff went into the Lone Eagle. Gus Porter was behind the bar, and three strangers were seated at one of the tables, their drinks in front of them.

"You men riding those Slash S horses out there?" asked Sheriff Cantwell.

"Yeah, Sheriff," said one of the men. "Why, what's the trouble?" All three of the men were unshaven and were rough-looking customers.

"Just this," spoke up Lane, "those horses belong to me."

"Well, now, kid, that's just your tough luck; we left our broncs in exchange for them," said the biggest of the three.

"Why did you make the exchange?" asked the sheriff.

"Well, Sir, it's like this; I'm a U.S. marshal and these are my deputies. Our horses were worn out and we were in a hurry," the big man said. "We're on the trail of some outlaws; switches like that are made all the time."

"Why didn't you come to the house and let me know what you were up to?" asked Lane.

The big man got to his feet, and the others followed suit.

"Look, young fellow, I don't have to explain my business to you, I told you that we were in a hurry, and that's all I'm going to tell you!" the big man said.

"You say that you're on the trail of outlaws," said Sheriff Cantwell. "Who are they?"

"Brady Hatch and his gang," said the big man. "From

what I've been told, this is where that outlaw-gunman used to hang out."

"What outlaw?" asked the sheriff.

"Wasn't this where Morgan Streeter lived?" asked the big man.

"Mister, you're mixed up somewhere; Morg Streeter was my dad, and he never was an outlaw," spoke up Lane.

"That ain't the way we heard it!" jeered the big man.

"Then you heard wrong," said the sheriff. "What are your names anyway?" he asked.

"I'm U.S. Marshal Preston Yarnell," said the big man. "These other men are Dab Shirey and—"

"My name is Val Ginter," spoke up the third man.

"Yarnell, I don't know where you got your information about Morg Streeter, but you're all wrong," said Sheriff Cantwell. "Morg Streeter was sheriff of this town, and he cleared all the outlaws out of here."

"The way I heard it was that he had a real racket going here, and everybody was scared of his reputation, and wouldn't do anything about it," sneered Yarnell.

The three men walked outside, followed by the sheriff and Lane.

"Are you stating that as a fact, or just what you heard?" asked Lane.

"Take it anyway you want, sonny, and if you don't like it, that's tough!" said Yarnell.

"Now let's not get too hasty here," said the sheriff. "You said you were after Brady Hatch and his gang. They tried to hold up the bank here in town and are now in prison."

"How many were there?" excitedly asked Ginter.

"We were able to get four of them, but we believe two others were involved," said the sheriff.

"From the information we got, there were only four of

them, so you got them all," said Ginter. "Hey, boss, where are the horses we traded for?"

"I switched your saddles back on your own broncs," said Lane.

"Kid, you're really trying to get your nose bumped, aren't you?" asked Yarnell. "Supposing you just get those horses back here and switch them back."

"What for, Mister? According to your statement about you being after the Hatch gang, you won't need them now; the Hatch gang is in jail," said the sheriff.

"Oh, yeah, that's right," said Yarnell. "Well, kid, you just got by this time, and by the skin of your teeth."

"That's what you say, Mister, but I'm still not satisfied with what you said about my dad," stated Lane. "Let me put you straight about how I feel since you said for me to take it any way I want. If you are making the statement that my dad was crooked, then I'll tell you to your face, you are a liar! Now, you can take that any way you want!"

The big man's face turned a brick red, and his lip curled back in a snarl. He threw his right fist in a round-house swing at Lane's jaw. Lane's left hand caught his wrist. Yarnell tried to pull his hand away from Lane's grip. A look of utter amazement appeared on his face, and then fear. Lane applied more pressure and Yarnell suddenly screamed and dropped to his knees. Lane twisted Yarnell's arm back until he fell over on his back. Lane stood over him and asked, "Are you ready to take back what you said?"

"Yes, yes, I didn't mean anything by it!" stammered the big man.

"I think you boys had better get out of town," suggested the sheriff.

The three men mounted up and hurried out of town.

The sheriff and Lane watched them go, the sheriff with a puzzled look on his face.

"Now, what do you suppose those men were doing here?" asked the sheriff.

"They said they were after the Hatch gang," said Lane.

"They were lying, son," said the sheriff. "That man wasn't Preston Yarnell; I've known Preston for years."

"Now, that is a puzzle," said Lane.

"Maybe I'm getting too suspicious, with all the happenings of the last few weeks, but I'm wondering about that man who said his name was Val Ginter. Did you notice that when that big fellow was naming those other men, that Ginter cut him off short, and gave his own name?" asked Sheriff Cantwell.

"I never caught it at the time, but, yes, you're right," said Lane. "Now, why would he do that?"

19

Monday, June 5th, was the date of Web Stocker's, alias Lefty Bowens, trial. The courtroom was again crowded. This was one of the biggest events ever held in Haleyville. The nearer the date grew, the more it was talked about. Ed Landers's store was one of the favorite gathering places for the residents of the town. Lettie Hallowell, Blaine's wife, asked Ed if he thought Stocker would hang for the crime.

"Lettie, I just don't know; it happened so many years ago that people tend to forget," said Ed. "On the other hand, Judge Warren is a pretty strict man on things of this nature. I guess we'll just have to wait and see."

Now the time was here. Judge Warren called the court to order, and when there was complete silence, he got to the matter at hand.

"As you folks already know, the prisoner, Web Stocker, has already confessed that he was guilty of the crime of murder; namely, shooting Morgan Streeter in the back. Normally, we would go through the process of a trial. However, Mr. Stocker has stated that he would allow me as judge to pronounce sentence on him."

A murmur went through the courtroom. The judge held up his hand for order.

"This is not a decision that I have come by lightly," said the judge. "I have deliberated many hours on this. Now, I have reached this decision: that, despite the passage of many years since this crime was committed, it does not take away the seriousness of this crime. A wife was deprived of the companionship of her husband; two children were robbed of their father's influence; this town was without a sheriff; and many of you folks were deprived of a friend. With all these things taken into account, I hereby sentence the defendant, Web Stocker, to be hanged two weeks from today. Are there any questions?"

The courtroom exploded in an uproar. Everybody was trying to talk at once. The judge once more signaled for order. The hubbub soon quieted.

"Does the prisoner have anything to say?" asked the judge.

"You better make sure they hang me, Judge!" he snarled, "because, if I get loose, I'm coming for you!"

Martha Streeter was sobbing quietly, and Lane was trying to console her. Judge Warren came down from his bench and approached her.

"Martha, I'm very sorry you had to sit through this; I know this has been hard on you," said Judge Warren. "Furthermore, I want you to know that my decision was based only on the facts; it had nothing to do with the fact that Morg was my friend, or how you might feel about it."

"I'm sure of that, Judge," she said. "I appreciate everything you've done."

"I did only what I had to do, my dear," he stated. "I felt it was the right decision,"

Lane was surrounded by people wanting to ask him questions. Hi Walker was one of those.

"Lane, do you agree with the judge's decision?" he asked.

"Well, I guess I have to," said Lane. "After all, he's more qualified than I could ever be to make a decision like that."

"Were you hoping that Stocker would hang?" asked Blaine Hallowell.

"No, not really," said Lane. "I was ready to go along

with whatever decision the judge made."

"I'm glad to hear that," said Blaine.

Lane, along with his mother and Callie, walked over to the hotel dining room. Abby Mason immediately came over and hugged Martha.

"I just heard the decision, and I know this had to be hard on you, Martha," she said.

"I'm certainly glad it's over," said Martha. "Maybe now we can get back to living again. I've been all upset since all this evidence came to light."

Lane, in an effort to alleviate the tension, spoke up. "Well, trot out the biggest steak you have, Aunt Abby; it's time to punish my stomach again."

"Martha, I'm afraid you're going to have to take a bull whip to him again," she said.

They all laughed, glad that the tensions of the day were past. Later, after the meal was over and the proper good-byes had been said, the Streeters got in the buggy to head for home. Sheriff Cantwell stopped them as he came up to the buggy.

"Martha, I'm certainly glad this is over. How do you feel about the decision?" he asked.

"Sheriff Cantwell, I really don't know," she said. "Everything is still going around in my head. But I want you to know that I deeply appreciate everything you've done. You did a fine job in accumulating all that evidence."

"Only my job, Martha," he stated. "Lane, Callie, how do you feel about it?" Lane looked at Callie, waiting for her to speak.

"I don't know, Sheriff," she said, "I don't fully understand it all."

"That's understandable, honey," he said. "How about you, Lane?"

"I feel bad that Lefty feels as he does about it," said Lane. "What could make him hate my dad the way he did?"

"That's something we'll never understand," said the sheriff. "Some men go bad for some reason that's all their own. I've never been able to figure it out."

"Well, thanks again for all you've done," said Lane. "Time we were getting home."

20

Three men sat around a campfire west of Haleyville. They were discussing the events of several days ago.

"Gib, I don't think that marshal bit you tried to pull fooled that sheriff at all," said one of the men, Dab Shirey by name.

"Bah, that sheriff don't know nothing!" said the big man, who thought he had passed himself off as Preston Yarnell, U.S. marshal.

"What about that kid, that Streeter, do you think he got wise?" asked the other man, who had given his name as Val Ginter.

"Nah, he was just mad because we had his horses," said Gib. "But I'll tell you one thing; I'm not finished with him. No man can do to me what he did and get away with it."

"Where were Lee and Lefty?" asked Val. "I didn't see hide nor hair of them."

"Beats me," said Shirey. "What do you aim to do about that kid, Gib?"

"I have a plan," said Gib. "But don't fool yourself; that kid is as strong as a horse." He held up his arm and pulled up his sleeve. A dark, purple ring showed around his wrist. "See what I mean?"

"He might be strong, but I'll bet you Lee can take him" said Val. "That brother of mine is the strongest man I've ever seen."

"What is this plan of yours, Gib?" asked Shirey.

"Just this: some night we'll sneak into his barn and hide," said Gib. "When he comes out, we'll jump him."

"You mean—kill him?" asked Shirey.

"No, nothing like that," said Gib. "We'll get the drop on him, take his gun if he's armed, put our guns down, and then beat him senseless. Did you see that big, black horse he was riding? Well, I want that horse."

"I'd like to have that Appaloosa myself," said Val. "That's a lot of horse."

"We can take whatever horses we want," said Gib. "We know where he keeps them."

"I'm still curious about Lee and Lefty," said Val. "You don't suppose that sheriff was lying, do you? Maybe he has Lee and Lefty locked up, too."

"Nah, he said they just got the four of them," scoffed Gib. "Don't worry; they'll show up."

"If we would have had more time in town, we could have got more information," said Shirey, "but that kid queered that."

"Well, we'll queer him good!" said Gib. "He's just a snot-nosed kid!"

"Did you know his old man?" asked Shirey.

"Nah, I never saw him, but they tell me he was pure poison with a gun," said Gib.

"Well, how are we going to work this about the kid?" asked Val.

"Like I said, we'll get the drop on him. Tell you what," said Gib, "I'll get a gun on him, and each of you boys grab an arm. I'll put my gun down, and we'll go to work on him."

"What if someone shows up?" asked Val.

"Then we'll pretend we're there to see about buying horses, and wait for another time," said Gib.

*   *   *

"What do you have planned for today, Lane?" asked Martha.

81

"Renny's coming over about eight o'clock and we're going to drive fifty of the unbroken stock into town to ship to Abilene to the K-R Ranch," said Lane. "You remember Ken Rader, the owner? He's going to be in town to pay me and inspect the horses."

Martha put their breakfast on the table. Callie came in and they sat down. Martha said, "Callie, would you say grace, please?"

Callie did so, and Lane, with an impish grin on his face, said, "Why, Callie, you forgot to pray for Renny."

"Oh, you think you're so smart!" she said.

After putting away an ample breakfast, Lane put his hat on, kissed his mother, and chucked Callie under the chin.

"See you later, twerp," he said. "By the way, if Renny comes to the house for water, make sure you serve it to him; he likes it better if you serve it to him."

Callie wrinkled her nose at him, and then smiled. Lane walked out to the barn. He stopped on the lower level where the horses were kept and threw down some hay. Midnight nickered softly and Lane rubbed his nose. He got a can and put a substantial amount of grain into the feed box in each stall. He walked up the stairs and went through the doorway.

"Well, well, look what we have here," jeered a voice behind him.

Lane turned to be confronted by the three men he had seen in town. The largest man had a gun leveled at him.

"Stand just so," ordered the big man. "Dab, make sure he don't have a gun."

"Are you men storing up more trouble for yourselves?" asked Lane.

"Not much trouble," said Gib. "We just aim to work

you over a little, is all. All right, boys, grab his arms."

Shirey and Ginter got in front of him and each grabbed an arm. Gib walked over and laid his gun on a bin with the other men's guns. Gib then placed himself in front of Lane. "This is to teach you a lesson; you'll find out you're just a kid and not to get smart with your betters. All right, boys, hold his arms back out of the way."

Gib drew back his right fist and swung viciously at Lane's head. As he did, Lane swung his arms together, with the men trying to hold on. Gib's fist, intended for Lane, instead struck Shirey, knocking him to the barn floor. Lane, with his left arm, now free, smashed a whistling left hook to the jaw of Ginter, who collapsed without a sound. Before Gib could get clear from Shirey's legs, Lane grabbed him with both hands, raised him over his head and slammed him viciously to the floor. He then grabbed Shirey, raised him to his feet, and drove his right fist into the man's mouth. Shirey went backward, hitting his head on the barn floor. The only one of the three who was stirring was Gib, and he was moaning softly.

"Wow, what's going on?" asked a voice.

Lane turned to see Renny, who had just appeared in the doorway.

"Oh, these fellows just wanted to wrestle a little, is all," said Lane. "We were just getting started, and they quit on me."

Lane went down to the lower level and got a big can of water. He threw water on all three of the men. Gib sputtered and tried to sit up. Lane took him by the arm and helped him to his feet. Renny was bending over Dab Shirey, whose mouth and lips were horribly mashed and swollen. Lane took the men's guns and extracted the shells from them. He walked over to where Val still lay on the floor. He was unconscious, his jaw swollen to twice the normal size. By now, Gib was able to maintain himself on his feet.

"Where are your horses?" asked Lane.

"Tied down in back of the barn," mumbled Gib.

"Renny, would you get their horses for them?" asked Lane.

"Sure thing, Lane," said Renny, his eyes as big as saucers.

By the time Renny was back with the horses, Ginter was on his feet. Lane handed them their guns.

"That's the second time you guys tried to run a sandy on me," Lane said. "I could have you thrown in jail, but I'm going to let you go. Remember this—if you ever mess with me again, I won't be so easy on you. I'd advise you to get out of town and stay out. Incidentally, you weren't fooling Sheriff Cantwell either. He's a friend of Marshal Yarnell."

None of the men said anything; they just mounted their horses and rode away.

21

Lee Jorms sat in the doctor's office while Doc Baldwin was busy removing the wires from his jaw. The procedure was somewhat painful, and Jorms winced several times. Finally, the last wire was taken out. Doc carefully wiped the few drops of blood that had seeped out.

"There you are, as good as new," said Doc. "I know that has to be a relief to get those out of there."

Jorms worked his jaw up and down a few times. His face still retained a few yellowish spots.

"I wouldn't get in any more scraps for a few days," said Doc. "Your jaw is healed, but that area will be tender for some time."

"Any scraps I get in with that kid will be with a gun!" retorted Jorms. "I owe him plenty!"

"Mister, let me give you some good advice," countered Doc Baldwin. "If you think Lane is good with his fists, you ought to see him work a gun. I saw his dad in action, but his dad never saw the day that he could match Lane with a gun."

"That so?" asked Jorms. "Well, we'll see. What do I owe you, Doc?"

"Oh, I think twenty-five dollars would cover it," said Doc.

Jorms paid him and stalked out of the office. On the way out, he encountered three men coming in.

"Lee!" ejaculated one of them.

"Val," returned Jorms, "what are you doing here?"

"Lee, meet Gib Hollis and Dab Shirey; Dab's nose might be broken," said Val.

Doc, hearing the commotion, opened his office door.

"Something I can do for you gentlemen?" he asked.

"Yeah, we want you to look at Dab's nose," spoke up Gib.

The men followed Doc into the office.

"What happened to your jaw, Val?" asked Lee Jorms. "It's all swollen."

"We'll explain later, Lee," said Val.

Doc was by now wiping the blood off Shirey's nose and mouth.

"You look like you been kicked by a horse, fellow," said Doc. "What happened?"

"We got in a little ruckus," said Hollis. "Nothing serious."

"You don't look too good yourself," said Doc, speaking to Gib. "Who have you boys been tangling with?"

"Never mind that, Doc; just patch him up so we can get out of here," said Hollis.

"Well, his nose is broken all right," said Doc. "This is going to take a little time."

Later, when Doc was finished, they walked out of the office. Shirey had a large bandage on his nose.

"Let's get a bite to eat," said Lee. "The hotel dining room has good food."

After the men were seated and their orders taken, Val said, "Gib, this is the brother I was telling you about. Say, Lee, where's Lefty? I haven't seen him since we hit town."

"He's in jail, Val, and that isn't all of it," said Lee. "He's going to be hanged in a few days."

"What? What did he do?" asked Val.

"Well, for one thing, his name is not Lefty Bowens; his real name is Web Stocker, and—"

"Web Stocker! Holy smoke!" spoke up Gib Hollis. "You mean the gunman?"

"None other," said Lee. "Well, you all know about

Morg Streeter; he used to be sheriff of this town. You remember how he was found dead? Well, Stocker was the one who shot him."

"You mean in a fair gunfight?" asked Hollis.

"Nah, he shot him in the back," said Lee Jorms.

"Well, what do you kn— Ssh! Here comes the waitress!" warned Gib.

Abby served them their food. "Will there be anything else?" she asked.

"We'll let you know," said Lee.

After she had gone back to the kitchen, Lee leaned close to the others and asked, "What was your trouble all about?"

A red-faced Gib Hollis started to explain. "You know that Morg Streeter you were talking about? Well, he has a son who has a horse ranch out of town a little ways. We went out there to beat the tar out of him, and it turned out all different than we thought. I'm ashamed to tell it, but he whipped all three of us."

"I told Gib and Dab that you could whip him pretty easily," said Val, who had passed himself off as Ginter.

"Well, since we're all being honest for a change, I guess you might as well know that he whipped me, too," said Lee.

"You're kidding!" said Val. "I didn't believe anybody could whip you."

"Remember when you saw me coming out of Doc's office?" asked Lee. "Well, he had just removed the wires from my jaw. That kid broke it when we got in a fight."

Just then Abby came out of the kitchen again. "Will you gentlemen be having any dessert?" she asked. They all refused, so she went back inside.

"How did that happen?" asked Val.

"We got in a row out in the street and, believe it or not,

I took a swing at him and missed; he grabbed me with one hand and lifted me off the ground. When he dropped me, he hit me, I think, with his right fist. That was the last thing I remembered until I came to," said Lee. "Make no mistake about it, that kid is as strong as a horse."

The men got up to go. Abby came out, and they paid their bill and left the dining room.

"Let's go up to my room," suggested Lee. They followed him up to his room.

"Now, just how did this all come about?" queried Gib.

Lee told them all about the plans for the robbery and how it had fizzled out.

"Well, how does this Web Stocker enter into all this?" asked Gib.

Lee further explained what had transpired at the trial, and how Sheriff Cantwell had brought up the findings on Stocker, alias Lefty Bowens.

"So help me, if Lefty hadn't blew his stack and admitted that he was guilty, I don't think they could have proved anything on him," said Lee. "I never knew he was Web Stocker until that sheriff brought it up."

"Are you going to try and spring him?" asked Val.

"I don't think I could," said Lee. "They're watching him like a hawk."

"Well, boys, I don't think there's anything here for us now," said Gib. "We may as well hit the trail."

"You boys can go if you want to," said Lee. "But I have a score to even up with that kid and the sheriff."

"How do you mean, even up?" asked Gib.

"Why, I'm going to kill that kid, and I'm also going to slap some sense into that big-nosed sheriff," said Lee.

"Well, Lee, no offense intended, but I don't mix in any murders," said Gib. "If you boys want to, that's up to you, but as for me, I'm riding."

"I'll ride with Gib," said Shirey. "How about you, Val?"

"Gib, if you don't mind, I think I'll stick here with Lee," said Val.

"That's fine with me," said Gib. "Be seeing you sometime."

22

Lane Streeter had come into town to see about some feed he had ordered. He heard a banging and hammering up behind the sheriff's office and he went to investigate. He found three men building a scaffolding to be the gallows for Web Stocker's hanging. Sheriff Cantwell was more or less supervising things.

"Are you coming to the hanging, Lane?" asked the sheriff.

"I wasn't planning to," said Lane.

"I'm glad to hear that, boy," said Sheriff Cantwell. "It shows you have no hard feelings. But, if you don't mind, I wish you would be here."

"Any particular reason, Mr. Cantwell?" asked Lane.

"Yes, there is, Lane," said the sheriff. "I'm a little concerned about that fellow, Jorms. He may try to break Stocker out of jail, or something."

"Do you have any others alerted?" asked Lane.

"Yes, I asked Gil Evans and Lafe Budrow if they would be willing to help, so they will both be here," said the sheriff.

"I guess I can be here," said Lane, "but I don't want Mother or Callie to see the hanging."

"I don't blame you; that's nothing for any woman to see," said Sheriff Cantwell. "Maybe your mother can put this all behind her once this is over."

"I sure hope so," said Lane. "Many is the time I've seen her crying over what happened."

The day of the hanging dawned bright and clear. Lane announced to his mother that he was going into town.

"You aren't going to the hanging, are you, Lane?" she asked.

"Mom, I hadn't planned to go, but Sheriff Cantwell asked me to be there," he answered.

"Why would he want you there?" she asked.

Lane explained what the sheriff had told him. "You know, Mom, I would rather you and Callie would go along with me, but I don't want you to go to the hanging," he said.

"Why do you want us to go with you?" she asked.

"I don't trust that fellow, Jorms; he's going to figure that I might be at the hanging, and he's liable to try and sneak in here to get even with me," he said.

"All right, Lane, we'll go along if you say so," she answered. "We'll stay with Abby at the dining room."

Lane hitched up the buggy for his mother and Callie. He saddled Midnight, as he didn't know when he might need him.

The town was packed with people. John Redfield and his sons were there.

"Lane, we wanted to be here in case that fellow Stocker has any friends with some funny ideas about interfering with this hanging," said John.

"I'm sure Sheriff Cantwell will be happy about that," said Lane. "That's why he asked me to come in."

"Lane, I was never one to talk about what happened years ago, but your father and I were very close friends," said John. "And I want you to know also that I'm proud of the way you have made a go of this business."

"Thank you, Mr. Redfield," said Lane, "I really appreciate friends like you and your family."

Just then Sheriff Cantwell appeared with Gil Evans leading Web Stocker up to the gallows. Reverend Manning walked along behind them.

"I don't need no sky-pilot around me!" snarled Stocker.

"Very well, just as you wish," said Reverend Manning.

All three men went up the steps. Sheriff Cantwell placed the noose around Stocker's neck.

Judge Warren appeared, carrying a written statement with him. He, too, mounted the platform. He began to read: "By the authority vested in me as judge of this territory, I have ordered this execution to be carried out. Mister Stocker, do you have any last words?" he asked.

"You can all go to — for all of me!" he snarled again.

"Very well, proceed, Sheriff," said the judge. "May God have mercy on your soul."

The other men stepped back from the trapdoor. Sheriff Cantwell went in back and released the latch holding the trapdoor. Stocker's body shot downward to be stopped with a loud THUNK. Lane shuddered and bowed his head. He had never witnessed anything like this before. He suddenly felt a great compassion for Stocker that he didn't know he was capable of experiencing. He suddenly turned and walked away. He felt an arm thrown around his shoulder.

"Things like this are never pleasant, boy, but sometimes they are necessary." He looked up to see John Redfield standing beside him. His throat was so constricted he could hardly speak.

"I find I don't hate him at all," Lane stammered. "In fact, I feel sorry for him."

"That's to your credit, boy," said John. "I think we all feel sorry for him now."

Roy Phillips, the town mortician, came driving up with his horse-drawn hearse. He went over to the sheriff. "Here's the coffin you ordered, Sheriff," he said.

The coffin was a pine box, as was the custom of the

day. The sheriff thanked Roy and said to Doc Baldwin, "Doc, do you think it's okay to take the body down now?"

"I think so," said Doc.

Several men helped Sheriff Cantwell remove Stocker's body from the gallows. Doc checked to see if Stocker was, in fact, dead.

"He's all yours, Roy," Doc said.

Roy supervised the placing of the body into the coffin, and the loading onto the hearse. He then drove off toward the town cemetery with some men he retained for such purposes.

Sheriff Cantwell came over to Lane. "Thank you for coming, Lane," he said. "I guess nothing happened after all."

"I'm glad it didn't," said Lane. "Sheriff, I guess I just never realized how many responsibilities a sheriff has. I was too young to understand all that Dad had to do. I wonder if I could spring that trapdoor if I had to. My admiration for you continually grows."

"We do what we have to do, Lane," said the sheriff. "If there's any crying to do, we do it in the tomorrows, and go on with life."

"Well, there's one thing sure," said Lane, "I would never want to be a sheriff."

The sheriff smiled. "Your calling seems to be with horses, and you're doing a fine job of it. Changing the subject a little, son; if I were you, I would kind of keep my eyes open. Jorms has left town and one of those other men was with him. I wouldn't trust him as far as I could throw him."

"Thanks, Mister Cantwell, I'll remember that," said Lane. "Well, I've got to get Mom and Callie and get home."

23

"Boy, Mom, look at this!" said Lane excitedly, holding up a telegram.

"What is it?" asked Martha.

He extended the telegram toward her. She took it and read it.

"Why, Son, that's wonderful!" she said. "Do you have that many that are broken?"

A boy had been sent out from town with the telegram. The U.S. Army wanted one hundred broken horses as soon as Lane could have them ready.

"Yes, Mom, we do; but they must meet the Army's specifications. I'm to wire them back and let them know if I can fill their order. They will send some troopers here to pick them up. Mom, they pay one hundred twenty-five dollars per horse," Lane said. "I'm going into town to send the wire now."

He went to the barn where he hastily saddled Midnight. Renny was working at a chore in the barn.

"Renny, we're really going to be busy for the next few days," he said. "I'm going into town and send a wire to the Army. While I'm gone, you can start separating the broken stock."

"How do you mean, separating them?" asked Renny.

"Here's where we're lucky that we don't have any culls," said Lane. "But the Army won't take any horse over fifteen two hands. As soon as I get back, I'll help you. And, Renny, there's a bonus in this for you. Out of the check, one hundred dollars is yours."

"Wow, Lane, that's a lot of money!" said Renny. "I don't expect you to do that."

"Don't worry; you're going to earn it," said Lane, smiling, as he took off for town.

Lane sent his wire. The next several days were hectic, with all the details he had to attend to. The following Monday, they had one hundred horses ready and waiting.

"What time will they be here?" asked Renny.

"They said around ten o'clock," said Lane.

About five minutes later they saw six blue-clad troopers riding up.

"Is your dad at home?" asked one of the troopers, addressing Lane.

"My father's dead," said Lane, smiling.

"Sorry about that," said the trooper. "Is this the Streeter Horse Ranch?"

"Yes, it is," answered Lane.

"Well, is the owner here, or someone in charge?" asked the trooper.

"You're looking at him," said Lane, extending his hand. "I'm Lane Streeter, and this is my rider, Renny Barker."

The lieutenant smiled and shook hands with both of them. "I expected someone a little older," he said.

"Afraid I can't accommodate you there, sir. We have your horses all ready for you," said Lane. "Follow us, please."

Lane mounted Midnight and led the troopers out down the lane toward the big pasture.

"Where did you get that horse, young fellow?" asked one of the other troopers.

"I caught him a few years ago," answered Lane.

"That's the most horse I ever saw," said another of the troopers.

"May I call you Lane?" asked the lieutenant.

"Please do," said Lane.

"You understand we can't accept any culls," said the lieutenant.

"You won't find any culls in this bunch, sir," said Lane. "We separate all the culls and turn them loose."

"I hope you're right," said the lieutenant, skeptically.

By now they were at the pasture where the horses were kept. All the men dismounted.

"This is Doctor Corning, our vet," said the lieutenant, pointing to one of the troopers.

Lane extended his hand. "Glad to meet you, sir," he said. "I'm sure you will find everything in order."

"Well, son, if there are no culls, it will be the first time in my career," said the vet.

The inspection of the horses was very time-consuming. The Army vet knew his business, and was very thorough. At the end of the first half hour, he had checked twenty horses.

"Well, Lieutenant, so far I haven't found one animal that isn't top grade," he remarked. "Where did you find all these horses, young fellow?"

"Some of them I bred from the best stock, but most of them Renny and I caught on the open range," said Lane.

"Where did you learn so much about horses?" asked the vet. "It's one thing to catch a horse, but it's another to know which to keep."

"My dad taught me a lot about horses, and after his death, Cappy Swinson, who worked for Dad, taught me what he knew," said Lane.

"I didn't know your dad, but I did know Swinson," said the vet. "He knew more about horses than any man I ever knew." After another hour, the vet was completed with his inspection. He shook his head in disbelief. "Well, it's just like you said; there are no culls," he said, with a smile on his face. "That's the first time I've ever seen that."

"Whom do you want this check made out to?" asked the lieutenant.

"Just make it out to Lane Streeter," answered Lane.

"Lane, forgive me for being curious, but do you run this ranch by yourself?" asked the lieutenant.

"Renny and I run it together," said Lane. "He may be young, but I couldn't ask for a better hand."

Renny modestly explained, "I just do what Lane tells me; he knows more about horses than anyone I know."

"C'mon down to the house; it's easier writing there," said Lane, "and besides, Mom will have some lemonade to cool you off."

"That sounds good to me," said the lieutenant. "We can come back for the horses later."

The troopers all followed Lane and Renny down to the big ranch house where they were ushered into the spacious living room.

"Mom, you are looking at eight very thirsty people," said Lane. "I'll let the lieutenant make the introductions."

"Please excuse me," said the lieutenant. "I never even gave you my name. I am Lieutenant Hatfield; Doctor Corning, and troopers Callahan, Bobst, Parks, and Newman."

"I am very happy to make your acquaintance," said Martha. "And this is my daughter, Callie."

All the men acknowledged the introductions in a rather embarrassed fashion. Martha poured lemonade for all the men. Lieutenant Hatfield wrote out a check for twelve thousand five hundred dollars and handed it to Lane.

"Thank you, Lieutenant, it's been a pleasure doing business with you," said Lane.

"The pleasure is all mine, Lane. Incidentally, we will

probably be needing more horses next year, if you can provide them," said the lieutenant.

"Just wire me when you need them, and we'll have them ready," said Lane.

The troopers left and went to collect the horses for the long haul back to Fort Ryan. Lane turned to his mother. "Mom, this calls for a celebration. I'll take you into town for dinner. Renny, you get your mother and bring her in and we'll meet you at the dining room."

"What about me?" asked Callie. "Don't I count?"

With an impish grin on his face, Lane said, "What do you think, Renny? Should we take her along?"

"Darn you, Lane, you set that up on purpose!" said Renny.

Lane chuckled and said, "Well, I guess we had better take her along then. Tell you what, Callie, you can even sit beside Renny."

"Oh, you think you're so smart!" retorted Callie. "I suppose you'll have to stop and pick up Elaine."

"That's telling him, Callie," said Renny.

Lane winked at both of them. "Do you think we ought to ask Sheriff Cantwell to join us? That would probably make Mom happy."

"Now don't you start in on me, or I'll get the broom after you," said Martha, laughing heartily.

When they all got to town, Lane went straight to the bank to deposit the check he had received from the lieutenant. He withdrew some money and walked to the sheriff's office. Sheriff Cantwell was seated outside, enjoying the cool breeze.

"What's on your mind, son?" he asked. "You look like the cat that's just swallowed the canary."

"Mister Cantwell, we'd like you to join us for dinner

at the dining room," he said. "There's just Mom, Callie, Renny, and his mother. "

"That's very kind of you, Lane," he said. "I'll just take you up on that."

When they got to the dining room, Lane motioned for Renny to join him aside from the others. He drew one hundred dollars from his wallet. "Renny, here's the bonus I promised you," he said.

Renny was all flustered. "Lane, you don't have to do that," he said.

"Renny, you've earned it and more. Every job I give you is done to perfection. I've never heard you complain once and I'm sure proud to have you working for me," said Lane.

"Gee, Lane, I don't know what to say," said Renny, with tears in his eyes. "Thanks awfully."

"Forget it," said Lane. "Now, let's go and pester Aunt Abby."

24

Lane and Renny were about five miles from the ranch looking for more wild horses. Lane had known for some time about one big stallion that had a number of horses in his string.

"Are you going to catch Blackie also?" asked Renny. Blackie was the name that Lane had given the big stallion.

"No, we'll just take a bunch of his following," said Lane. "That way he can build up another bunch, all with good breeding stock."

It wasn't until the second day of looking that they found the herd. They came up on the horses away from the wind. "Look at him," said Lane, admiringly. The big horse stood apart from the rest of the herd, keeping watch over them. "Well, let's do it the way we always do."

They cut in on the herd and split it up so that the great majority of the horses were separated from the leader. They now started the horses running back toward the ranch. "Make them run as fast as they can!" yelled Lane. "We want them tired."

At first, they were hard-pressed to keep up with the galloping horses, but the pace began slowing after a few miles. They had prepared for the run by having a relay of horses tied at intervals along the route. As they would change horses, the spent horses would just join with the rest of the running herd. In a short time, they were back at the ranch. Lane cut ahead and opened the main gate. The new horses streamed into the pasture.

"How many do you think there are?" asked Renny.

"I'm guessing about sixty or seventy," said Lane.

After the horses had settled down and began grazing, they took a count.

"How many did you count?" asked Renny.

"I got sixty-seven; how many did you get?" asked Lane.

"I got sixty-six," said Renny. "Let's count them again."

"Your count is right," said Lane, "I got sixty-six this time."

"Now, the real work begins," said Renny. "They have to be broken. "

"Renny, I'm going to see if Buck Rawlins is available; he's a good bronc-stomper, and we're going to be too busy catching more horses to spend the time that it will take. I'll go over to see Cal Rowan first thing tomorrow, and see if we can borrow Buck," said Lane.

The next morning found Lane riding up to the C-R Connected Ranch. He found Cal Rowan out in the corral supervising a shoeing job.

"Morning, Lane, what are you up to? Did you drop by to see if you could palm off some more culls?" asked Cal, smiling.

"No, I hate to swamp the market," said Lane. "I lose too many customers that way. Cal, how busy is Buck Rawlins right now?"

"Well, you see him shoeing horses; he's not too busy. He's got all those horses broken that you sold me," said Cal. "Why? What did you have in mind?"

"Well, Cal, it's like this; the Army just bought one hundred horses from me, all broken stock. Renny and I have been pretty busy rounding up more horses, and we don't have the time to break them," said Lane. "We wondered if we could borrow Buck for about a month or so until we get caught up again."

"I don't see why not," said Cal. "In fact, I'll make you a deal; I loan you Buck, and instead of you paying him, just give me three of the horses you caught. Is that a bargain?"

"More than a bargain, Cal, and I'll go you one better," said Lane. "I'll give you five of the horses."

"Lane, you got a bargain. Buck will be over first thing in the morning."

Lane rode back to the ranch more than pleased. This would cut their work in half. Now he and Renny could spend their time catching as many horses as would be needed. A few months ago, Lane, while scouting some other horse herds, had seen a large gray stallion with quite a following. Lane estimated that there were close to one hundred twenty-five horses in that bunch. The next morning, after Buck Rawlins had arrived, and been made acquainted with what was needed, Lane and Renny started out to locate the herd. Just before noon, they found it. Using their usual method, they drove the horses to the pasture and, there, locked them in.

"How many did you count this time?" asked Lane.

"I got ninety-two," answered Renny.

"That's what I got," said Lane. "Well, tomorrow we'll separate the culls."

In the next two weeks, they captured more than five hundred new horses. Buck Rawlins had all the work he needed, but he never complained. "Lane, I don't know how you do it," he said. "I haven't found one cull in all these horses that I have ridden."

"We separate them when we catch them, and let them go," explained Lane. "I figger it saves time in the long run."

"You're right, it would," said Buck. "But I'm going to tell you something; not many guys your age have the savvy to know which ones to keep."

"You get used to it as you go along," answered Lane.

"Well, you sure got a fine business going here," said Buck. "There's some stock here that any man would give his eyeteeth to own. I saw an Appaloosa in the other pen over there that is as fine a horse as I ever saw."

"He was in a bunch that we drove in one day," said Lane. "How he got there, I'll never know. He wasn't branded, so I slapped my brand on him."

"Don't blame you," said Buck. "Well, I got work to do."

At the end of two months, Lane figured that they had enough stock for a while, so he began gentling the horses that he would sell as broken stock. Buck, after eating breakfast on the morning he was to leave, said to Martha, "Ma'am, I purely don't know when I've tasted better grub; them apple pies you bake are out of this world."

"Why, thank you, Buck, and come back anytime; it's been a pleasure having you here," said Martha, smiling.

Lane and Buck went outside. "Buck, I suppose Cal told you the arrangement he and I made?" said Lane.

"Yep, he told me; you don't owe me a cent," said Buck.

"Do you suppose you could take his five horses with you?" asked Lane.

"Why, sure, no trouble at all," said Buck.

"All right, here's a bill of sale made out to him stamped paid," said Lane.

"And here's another one also stamped paid."

"What's that one for?" asked Buck.

"Come over here," said Lane. Buck followed him over to the barn. There, just inside the barn, stood the five horses for Cal. Along with them stood the Appaloosa. "He's yours, Buck."

"Man, I can't afford a horse like that!" exclaimed Buck.

"Buck, that horse is just going to waste here," said Lane. "You know as well as I do that for a horse to be any good for anybody, he has to be used. I have Midnight and I know you will be good to that horse; so, he's yours."

"Lane, I don't know what to say," stammered Buck. "Why, I—"

"Consider it said," Lane told him, "and thanks for all you've done."

Buck saddled up the Appaloosa and started home with his charges in tow.

25

Sheriff Josh Cantwell had been a cowboy for many years before becoming a deputy under Morg Streeter. He still had a great love for horses and, when there was nothing pressing in town, he liked to saddle his little mare, Squaw, and take a ride. On this day, he was riding past Blue Spring, about five miles west of Haleyville. He liked the water in this spring, as it was always very cool and refreshing. He dismounted and knelt at the spring.

"Now you just hold it right there the way you are, old man," said a voice behind him. He turned his head to see Lee Jorms and his brother, Val, standing beside him. The elder Jorms had a gun pointed at him. The sheriff stood up and raised his hands. "What's this all about, Jorms?" he asked.

"Remember what I told you once, Sheriff, that nobody sticks a gun in my ribs and gets away with it," Jorms said. "Well, this is pay day, and you do the paying!"

He reached over, lifted the sheriff's gun out of its holster, and tossed it aside. He then holstered his own gun and backhanded the sheriff in the face. Sheriff Cantwell went over backward. Jorms immediately dropped on him with bunched-up knees, driving all the breath out of his lungs. Jorms smashed him viciously in the face with his clenched fist. He struck him again and again. It was obvious that the sheriff was unconscious. Val grabbed his brother's wrist as he attempted to strike the sheriff again.

"Stop! Lee, you'll kill him!" exclaimed Val.

"It would serve him right!" snarled Lee.

He rose from his gruesome task and said, "Maybe

you're right; that'll teach him to interfere with me. The same goes for that kid, too! I'm not finished with him yet."

"Lee, I think we should ride out of here," said Val. "This is bad business, beating up this sheriff, and all. What do you have in mind for that Streeter kid?"

"I'll kill him if I have to!" snarled Lee. "Nobody, but nobody, does to me what he did!"

"What did he do? Just socked you on the jaw, is all," said Val. "He socked me on the jaw, too, but he was just defending himself. All three of us jumped him, and he whipped us. I don't hold it against him."

"You ought to try sipping soup for two months and see how you like it," said Lee. "He busted my jaw in three places and I could hardly talk, it hurt so bad. No, I'm not finished with him, not by a long shot!"

"Lee, I don't think you can whip him in a fair fight," said Val. "There was a time that I didn't think anybody could whip you, but I don't believe that anymore. When we three jumped him, I had him by the wrist and Shirey had him by the other wrist. He swung us around like we were pieces of paper. I'm telling you, I wonder if that guy is human."

"Well, we're going to find out," said Lee. "I'll get him one of these days."

"Lee, you don't want to kill anybody, do you?" asked Val.

"What do I care?" said Lee. "It wouldn't be the first guy I killed; I hit a guy in Tombstone once and broke his neck. It was him or me."

"Lee, I don't like it," said Val. "I've never killed anybody and I don't want to."

"You're just too soft, Val," jeered Lee. "If it's too rough on you, just ride out; nobody's holding you."

106

"What are you going to do about the sheriff?" asked Val.

"Let him lay; he'll come to after a while," said Lee. "C'mon, let's get out of here."

The two men rode off on their horses. After a space of about twenty minutes, the sheriff moaned softly and began to stir. He crawled to the water's edge and soaked his head in the cool water. He immediately felt better, but it was another thirty minutes before he could get on his horse and head back to town. It seemed like an eternity to him when he finally reached the livery stable. Hi Walker came out to greet him.

"I wondered when—holy mackerel, Sheriff, what happened to you?" asked Hi.

"Get Doc Baldwin for me, will you, Hi?" he asked.

Hi helped him down from his horse, lowered him into a chair, and headed for the doctor's office. In a few minutes, Hi and Doc Baldwin hurried into the stable. They found the sheriff lying on the floor, unconscious. Doc began examining him for damages. "I think he has some ribs broken, and he may have a concussion," said Doc. "Who did this to him?"

"I don't know, Doc, he just rode in and told me to get you," said Hi. "Will he be all right?"

"I think so," said Doc, "but it's going to be awhile before he gets back to normal. Hi, would you please go to my office and get the stretcher I keep there? You know where it is. I'll round up some men to help carry him to my office."

"Sure thing, Doc," said Hi. He hurried off on his errand.

Later that evening, when Doc had finished cleaning the sheriff up, he gave him a sedative to make him rest better. The sheriff had regained his senses by then, and wanted to talk.

"Who did this to you, Josh?" asked Doc.

"That Lee Jorms fellow," answered the sheriff. "His brother was with him, but he didn't take part in it. Everything was pretty hazy about then, but it seems like he was trying to get him to leave these parts. Now, I'm not real sure, but it seems like I heard Lee Jorms say that he was going to get the kid; I think he meant Lane Streeter. Somebody had better warn him."

"Somebody will, but, right now, Josh, you get some rest. You have at least three broken ribs and a mild concussion," said Doc Baldwin. "You'll have to take it easy for a few days."

The sedative began taking over then and the sheriff started nodding. Doc walked softly from the room. He walked out on the street with the intent of getting someone to ride out to the Streeter ranch to warn Lane of what the sheriff had told him. He saw Renny Barker riding by and hailed him. Renny rode over to him. Doc conveyed the information that Sheriff Cantwell had given him concerning Lane. Renny promised to let Lane know about it and rode off. Doc Baldwin walked over to the bank.

"Angie, is Blaine In?" he asked the teller.

"Yes, Doc, go right in; I know he'll want to see you," she answered.

Doc walked into Blaine Hallowell's office. They had been close friends for years.

"Well, Doc, what brings you here?" asked Blaine. "Here to borrow about a million?"

"No, nothing that trivial," said Doc, smiling. "Blaine, we have a problem. "

"What's that?" asked Blaine.

"That Jorms bird beat the living daylights out of the

sheriff," said Doc. "He broke three of his ribs and Josh also has a mild concussion."

"Why would he do something like that?" asked Blaine.

"Who knows," said Doc. "I think he's a little off his rocker, myself, but, at any rate, we are without a sheriff for a while."

"Where is Jorms now?" asked the banker.

"I don't know, but see what you make of this," said Doc. "Josh was pretty hazy after the beating, but he thinks he heard Jorms threaten Lane Streeter."

"You'd think he had enough of Lane, after what happened before," commented Blaine.

"Some men can't take a beating without getting even," said Doc. "What worries me is that he may try to get Lane from ambush."

"Has Lane been warned?" asked Blaine.

"Yes, Renny was in town and I told him to tell Lane about these threats," said Doc. "But what do we do for a sheriff until Josh recovers?"

"Maybe we won't need one before then, and, you know, maybe we could ask Lane to step in if we needed him," said the banker.

"I hope that won't be necessary," said Doc. "That would worry Martha sick."

"Yeah, you're right, Doc. Well, let's just keep our fingers crossed," said Blaine.

26

Lane noticed that Renny was pushing his horse rather hard on the way back from town. That was unusual for Renny, and Lane knew there must be a reason for it. As Renny thundered to a stop in front of Lane, it was obvious that he was excited about something.

"What's the big rush, Renny?" asked Lane. "You're all in a lather about something."

"Yeah, Lane, you're right!" said Renny. "Doc Baldwin told me to give you the news. You know that Lee Jorms guy? Well, he beat the daylights out of Sheriff Cantwell. He has broken ribs and a concussion. But Doc said to warn you. The sheriff overheard Jorms threaten you. Doc said for you to be careful and to keep your eyes open. "

"When did this happen?" asked Lane.

"This morning sometime," said Renny. "Gee, Lane, what are you going to do?"

"I don't know yet," said Lane. "First of all, I'm going in to see the sheriff, and I'll just go on from there. Did you get the staples I sent you in for?"

"Oh, yeah, they're in my saddlebags," said Renny, and, dismounting, he got a bag out of his saddlebags and handed it to Lane.

"Thanks, Renny," said Lane. "Tell you what, you just go ahead and fix that fence we were working on and I'll see you later. I'm going in now to see the sheriff and Doc."

Renny walked to the barn to get the necessary tools, and Lane went to the house to inform his mother about what had happened.

"Lane, you be careful," said Martha, after she had been apprised of the happenings.

"Don't worry, Mom," Lane said, buckling on his gun-belt, "I'll be back in a short time."

He saddled up Midnight, and headed for town. As he rode, he went over the situation in his mind. "Evidently that Jorms hasn't learned his lesson," he mused to himself.

Arriving in town, he went directly to Doc Baldwin's office, surmising that the sheriff would be there, as Doc kept his more serious patients in one of his rooms. Doc answered his knock.

"Come on in, Lane; I've been expecting you," said Doc.

"How's the sheriff?" asked Lane.

"Come see for yourself," said Doc. "He got a pretty bad going-over, but he's going to be all right. It's just going to take time."

He ushered Lane into the sheriff's room. Lane was shocked at his appearance. The sheriff's face was all discolored and his eyes were swollen nearly shut.

"How are you feeling, Sheriff?" Lane asked.

"Well, I've felt better in my time," said the sheriff, with a rueful grin on his face.

"How did this happen?" asked Lane.

"I was out riding and I stopped at Blue Spring to get a drink of water," said the sheriff. "As I knelt down to drink, this Jorms got the drop on me. I never knew he was there until he spoke. His brother was with him. Jorms took my gun and proceeded to knock me senseless. I don't think I was entirely out, for it seemed I could hear him talking. If I'm right, he was threatening to get even with you."

"Did his brother take part in the beating?" asked Lane.

"No, not if I remember correctly," said Sheriff

Cantwell. "In fact, I don't think he was too happy about the whole thing."

"Well, if Jorms shows his face around here again, I think we should throw him in jail," said Lane.

"I second the motion," said Doc Baldwin. "He's too dangerous to be running around loose."

"What can we charge him with, Mister Cantwell?" asked Lane. "I still think he and that Stocker were in that attempted bank robbery."

"So do I," said the sheriff, "but we can't prove it. All we can charge him with is assault and battery. I wasn't trying to arrest him, so we can't get him for resisting arrest."

"Well, you just get back on your feet again, and, if that bird shows up around here, we'll talk about it then," said Lane.

"I'll do my best," promised the sheriff. Lane and Doc Baldwin walked out to the street.

"Thanks for letting me see him, Doc," said Lane. "How long do you think it will be before he's on his feet?"

"I would say in about a week, but he won't be able to fork a bronc for some time yet," said Doc.

Lane headed back to the ranch and was surprised at how angry he was. *What a character that Jorms is*, he thought to himself. *Well, if I get another crack at him, I'll make him pay for the sheriff.*

He looked up to see Bob Holiday and Elaine approaching him. Bob was driving the buckboard.

"My, the man looks positively fierce," joshed Elaine. "Why all the dark looks? Did you stub your toe or something?"

Lane grinned. "Nothing so fierce as that," he said. Then in a more serious vein, he told them what had transpired.

"What's the matter with that Jorms fellow? Is he crazy

112

or something?" asked Bob.

"I don't know, Mr. Holiday, but I do know he's dangerous," said Lane. "After what happened on the street that day, I wouldn't let Elaine ride alone until this thing is settled."

"I think that's good advice," said Bob.

"I never want to meet that man again!" said Elaine, shuddering. "He gives me the creeps."

"He may be mentally ill or something," said Lane, "which doesn't help our problem."

"Not any," said Bob. "Well, I'll be seeing you, Lane; we got things to do."

"Yeah, me too," said Lane. "I'll be over Sunday, Elaine."

"Okay, Lane," she said, blowing him a kiss as they drove off.

27

The month of August was half gone, and the heat was beating down on Lane and Renny as they were working on more horses. Both of them were as brown as coffee. They had just ridden back to the barn when Lane noticed they had a visitor. It was Tom Redfield.

"Did you think I had forgotten about that bay I had ordered?" asked Tom.

"No, I figgered you would come and get him when you were ready," said Lane. "How are you feeling?"

"I'm about back to normal now," said Tom. "But I'll tell you something, the next time I tangle with that guy, it will be with a gun. I believe someone is going to have to do something about him after what happened to Sheriff Cantwell."

"You're right, Tom, that guy is really storing up trouble for himself," said Lane. "I've got the feeling we haven't seen the last of him."

Renny, who had gone to get the big bay, now arrived back with him. Tom took his saddle off the horse he had been riding and put it on the bay. He cantered around the enclosure a few times and nodded. "Boy, Lane, he sure is gentle; you sure have a way with horses," he said. "How old is he?"

"Well, he was a colt when I caught him, and we've had him here for about a year," said Lane. "He ought to last you quite a while."

"I sure hope so," said Tom, extending a check to Lane. "And, by the way, here's a telegram that came for you; I almost forgot it."

"Thanks, Tom," said Lane. "I wonder what this could

be about." Tearing open the envelope, he extracted the telegram and glanced at the message.

"Wow, Renny, we're going to be busy again!" Lane said. He handed the telegram to Renny.

"Boy, I'll say!" said Renny. "They'll be here on Monday."

Lane explained to Tom, who had a puzzled look on his face. "That was from the Army; they just bought one hundred horses from us and now they want forty more."

"Hey, that's great!" said Tom. "Well, good luck."

"Thanks, Tom, you've really made my day today," said Lane. "Give my best to your folks."

"I'll do that," said Tom, cantering off on the bay, with the other horse in tow.

Lane went to the house to give his mother and Callie the news.

"Why, Lane, that's wonderful!" said Martha.

"Does that mean we eat in town again?" asked Callie, smiling.

"If you want to, we can," said Lane, "but you have more up your sleeve than that."

"I just thought Mom could hold Mr. Cantwell's hand since he's feeling better." She grinned, with a conspiratorial look in her eye.

Lane grinned also. "That might cure him completely."

"Oh, you two!" Martha exclaimed. "You'll drive me to drink!"

Lane got behind his mother and, taking her by the elbows, lifted her over his head. She squealed and exclaimed, "You idiot, you put me down right now!"

Lane laughed and lowered her to the floor. "Why, Mom, you used to pick me up when I was small; now that you're smaller than me, why can't I pick you up?"

"Yeah, Mom, and besides, he's just practicing so he

can pick Elaine up the same way," said Callie, laughing.

"That's enough out of you, twerp," Lane said. "Any more and I'm going to call Renny in and see how high he can lift you."

"Don't you dare!" exclaimed Callie.

Lane went out the door, grinning. Renny was out at the pasture already separating the horses that they would need for the Army mounts. Lane looked over several that he had chosen. "Good, Renny, these are some that I would have chosen," he said. "I'm going to let you pick out all forty of them."

"What if I goof up?" asked Renny.

"You won't goof up," said Lane. "You know as well as I do which ones to pick." Lane went back to the barn to do another chore that needed doing. In about an hour, Renny came in also.

"All finished?" asked Lane.

"Yeah, I think so," said Renny. "But I want you to check them."

"What for?" asked Lane. "If they suit you, they suit me."

The following Monday morning they were waiting for the troopers to show up. Lane could see that Renny was very nervous, worrying about the horses he had chosen. Finally they came riding in. They were the same troopers as before with one exception. There was a colonel with them. Lieutenant Hatfield shook hands with Lane and introduced Colonel Watson to Lane.

"This is the commanding officer of Fort Ryan, Colonel Watson," said Lieutenant Hatfield.

"I'm happy to make your acquaintance, Colonel," said Lane.

"You are probably wondering why I came along," said

Colonel Watson. "When Lieutenant Hatfield told me about meeting you and that you were the son of Morg Streeter, I wanted to meet you and see your mother again. Your father and I were close friends years ago."

"Come on down to the house, and you can talk to Mom while Doctor Corning checks the horses," said Lane. "Would you please come also, Lieutenant, and also Doctor Corning?"

The four of them started for the house. Doctor Corning had a puzzled expression on his face "You probably wondered why I wanted you to come along," said Lane, chuckling. "Doctor Corning, Renny picked all of those broncs. When you check them over, start finding fault with them on one excuse or another. We'll have a little fun with Renny."

"Okay, I'll do it!" said the vet.

"You mean you let that young boy pick all those horses you are selling to us?" asked Colonel Watson.

"I know he's only fifteen, but you won't find any culls in this bunch either," said Lane.

They reached the house and Lane ushered them in. Martha came in from the kitchen. She looked at the men and suddenly her face lit up in a smile. "Why, you are Jim Watson!" she said, looking at Colonel Watson.

"How are you, Martha?" he said, extending his hand. "It's been a long time."

"It's Colonel Watson now, Mom," said Lane, grinning. "Well, should we get back to the horses?" Lane and Doctor Corning left the house and rode back to the pasture. The vet immediately dismounted and began checking the horses. He winked at Lane and began working. He checked seven of the horses and turned to Lane.

"What seems to be the trouble here, Lane?" he asked.

"None of these first seven could pass the Army inspection."

Lane glanced over at Renny. He was crestfallen and looked as though he was ready to burst into tears. Lane and Doctor Corning burst into laughter and the other troopers looked puzzled.

"We're just pulling your leg, young fellow," said Doctor Corning, laughing. "These horses are all top-flight."

"Darn you, Lane, you put him up to that!" said Renny, his face red.

"Guilty as charged," said Lane, grinning. "But if you could have seen the look on your face."

"He did look kind of downhearted, for a fact," said the vet. He completed his inspection of the horses and straightened up.

"Just like last time, not a cull in the bunch," said Doctor Corning. "Young fellow, you sure know your horses.

Renny looked pleased and said, "Thank you, sir."

Doctor Corning called to one of the troopers, "Sergeant Callahan, you are in charge; you men start the horses. I'll report to Lieutenant Hatfield and we'll catch up with you."

"Yes, Sir; all right, men, let's get them started," said Callahan.

Lane and Doctor Corning went back to the house. They went inside and Doctor Corning reported to Lieutenant Hatfield. "Everything's okay, sir. No culls this time either. The men have started back with the horses. I told them we would catch up with them."

"Fine, Doctor, fine. Were there forty as ordered?" asked the lieutenant.

"Yes, sir, forty, right on the nose." answered Doctor Corning.

Lieutenant Hatfield wrote out a check for five thousand dollars and handed it to Lane. "Thank you, sir," said Lane. "You folks are keeping Renny and me pretty busy."

"Well, Martha, this has been like old times," spoke up Colonel Watson. "And, young man, all I get is good reports on the horses you've been selling us."

"That's good news," said Lane, smiling. "Let us know when you want more, and we'll do our best to get them for you."

"We'll do that. Martha, take care, you hear?" said the colonel. "And thank you for your hospitality."

"The pleasure's been all mine, Jim," said Martha. "Please come back."

"I'll do that," said Colonel Watson. "And, now, we must be getting on the road."

After the men had left, Lane went into his office and wrote out a check. Martha came in and teasingly asked, "Lane, did you mean it when you told Callie you were going to treat us again?"

"I sure did mean it," he said. "And, Mom, I'm going to give Renny a check for forty dollars. He has earned it. Did you know that he picked out all forty of those horses?"

"Why, Lane, that's wonderful!" said Martha. "And I'm also glad that you're giving him that bonus."

Lane left the house, called Renny over to him, and handed him the check. "What's this?" asked Renny.

"Just your share of those horses we sold," said Lane. "Do you realize the horses we've sold here lately? From now on your pay will be forty dollars a month."

"But, Lane, that's more than a cowpuncher gets," objected Renny.

"Renny, I couldn't have done all this without your help," said Lane. "Now you just quit your fussing, get your mother, and meet us in town at the dining room."

Tears filled Renny's eyes. "How can I ever thank you?" he asked.

"Just by working the way you have been," said Lane, smiling.

28

Later that evening, after a sumptuous meal, Lane stopped at the jail. Sheriff Cantwell was sitting in his favorite chair in front of the jail.

"How are you feeling, Sheriff?" asked Lane. "Are you about back to normal again?"

"Yeah, just about," said the sheriff. "My ribs are still a little sore, but, aside from that, everything seems okay."

"I'm glad to hear that," said Lane. "Have you heard anymore about Jorms's whereabouts?"

"No, I haven't heard a thing, but you better believe he's around somewhere," said Sheriff Cantwell. "Don't forget that threat he made against you; I believe he meant every word of it."

"If only we knew where he might strike next, we could be better prepared," said Lane. "Do you have any ideas on where that might be?"

"No, I can't say as I have," answered the sheriff. "You can never tell about a guy like him; just when you least expect it, that's when he'll pull something."

"Well, I still think he was in on that holdup scheme," said Lane.

"That's the same way I feel, but the problem is, we can't prove it," answered the sheriff. "Sometimes I think he isn't all there mentally."

"Wouldn't that be true of any outlaw or anyone who breaks the law?" asked Lane.

"No, not really," said the sheriff. "Take that Brady Hatch, the bank robber, for instance; he's smart as a whip, but he's never killed anybody. He's not really vicious or even mean. He's as sane as anybody I know."

"What makes people like that go into a life of crime?" asked Lane.

"Son, if we knew the answer to that question, there would be a lot less crime," said the sheriff. "I doubt if anyone will ever find out what makes some men tick. This Jorms, for instance, is a different proposition. He's just plain vicious. The only way he'll change is when he's dead."

"That would make it final, all right," said Lane. "Well, I've got to get home; I'll keep my eyes open, Mister Cantwell."

Since Martha and Callie had driven into town in the buggy, Lane rode on home on Midnight. The setting sun was a sight to behold. Lane was in his glory. He had always loved the various changes that nature presented. Even as a little boy, he had wondered what life was all about. Seeing the sun dip below the far-off mountains filled him with awe.

"Lord, some artists can paint some beautiful pictures, but you top them all," he mused aloud.

As he neared the ranch, he slowed Midnight to a walk so that he might enjoy the evening sunset even more. As the sun was dropping over the distant horizon, he stopped the giant horse to get a better view.

"Is that you, Lane?" asked a voice out of the gathering gloom. Lane looked at two riders who were motionless. They were Cal Rowan and his foreman, Gil Robertson.

"Hi, Cal," said Lane. "What brings you up this way?"

"You know those horses you sold us?" asked Cal. "Well, five of them were stolen from the ranch last night, along with that Appaloosa you gave Buck Rawlins."

"What? Who would do a thing like that?" asked Lane.

"I don't know, but I sure aim to find out!" answered Cal. "And I might add that if I do find out, there's going to be some neck-stretching around here."

"We did find out that there were two men in on it," offered Gil.

"Lane, Sheriff Cantwell tells me that you are pretty good at reading sign, and I was wondering if you could make anything out of the tracks we found," said Cal.

"I'll sure try, Cal," said Lane. "It's too late to read any sign tonight, so why don't you and Gil spend the night here, and we'll take off first thing in the morning."

"I'd appreciate that, Lane," said Cal. "We'll take you up on it."

"C'mon in the house and we'll get you situated for the night," said Lane.

The three men went into the house. Martha and Callie were seated at the kitchen table.

"Mom, Cal and Gil are going to spend the night with us," said Lane.

"That's fine; how are you, Cal?" asked Martha. "Gil, how've you been?"

"I hope we're not intruding, Martha," said Cal.

"Not at all," Martha assured him.

Lane hastened to explain to his mother about the stolen horses. "We'll be wanting an early start in the morning, Mom," said Lane. "When Renny comes, let him know where I am and tell him to go ahead with what we were doing today; he'll know what that means."

The next morning Martha had breakfast ready for the men. After Gil had polished off his fifteenth pancake, Lane grinned at Cal. "Does he eat like this every day, Cal?" he asked.

"We don't get food like this every day," said Gil.

"Bones does a fair job, but he never saw the day he could cook like this." Bones Hadley was the flunky at the C-R Connected.

"Bones does pretty good, but he can't top you, Martha," said Cal, smiling. "But it does run me an extra fifty dollars a month to feed Gil."

"I can believe it," said Lane, grinning. "Mom says it takes just about that amount to feed Callie."

"Lane Streeter!" ejaculated Martha, "I never made a statement like that in my life."

All the men enjoyed a laugh at Callie's expense. Finished with breakfast, they all went out and saddled up. Just as they were leaving, Renny rode in. Lane gave him his instructions, and the three of them rode off, heading for the C-R Connected.

"Let's go through town," suggested Cal. "Bones needs a few supplies."

While Cal was in the store, Lane noticed a number of horses in front of the sheriff's office. As they were passing the office later, the door opened and John Redfield stepped out with two of his sons. Sheriff Cantwell followed them and shut the door.

"Shouldn't you tell Sheriff Cantwell about those horses, Cal?" asked Lane.

"Good idea," agreed Cal. "Sheriff, I had some horses stolen the other night, and we're on our way to see if Lane could pick up their sign."

"You, too, Cal?" spoke up John Redfield. "That's why I'm here; somebody made off with some of my horses last night."

"Dad, you don't really know when they were taken," offered Tom Redfield.

"No, that's true," agreed John. "We found it out this morning."

"I have a suggestion," said the sheriff. "Cal, you and your group see what you can find out at your place, and I'll go out with John and his boys and see what we can find out there."

The parties split up and went their separate ways. As the sheriff and the Redfield contingent neared the Rocking R, Tom Redfield spoke up.

"Sheriff, why did Cal have Lane with him?" he asked.

"That boy is just like his dad," said Sheriff Cantwell. "He can track a snake upstream."

"How come we never knew these things about him?" asked Tom. "I mean, we just took it for granted that he was just Lane Streeter, and here the guy is strong as a horse and nobody knew it. Now we find he has other talents as well."

"The thing I like about him the most is that if he doesn't know something, he'll ask," said the sheriff. "Some people will try to bluff it through, but not Lane."

"What I like about him also is his honesty," said John. "Every horse he has sold me is the best stock. He doesn't try to sell any culls."

"What is this, hurrah for Lane Streeter Day?" asked Andy Redfield, laughing. "If it is, I may as well add my two cents' worth; what I like about him is that he's so full of fun, and can laugh at himself."

"You know, as young as he is, he's become a pretty important person in this community," offered Sheriff Cantwell. "Doesn't he seem older than he really is?"

"That's because he has a good head on his shoulders," said John. "How many people do you know who could have taken over that business and made it a paying business?"

"That's true, John," said the sheriff. "Well, here we are; now let's see what we can find."

John led them down to the pasture where the horses had been kept. The sheriff got down from his horse and very carefully scanned the ground. He looked puzzled about something. "Were any of those horses shed that you had stolen?" he asked John.

"No, we hadn't got around to it yet," answered John. "Why do you ask?"

"Then there were two riders in on the steal," answered the sheriff.

"How do you know that?" asked Andy. "It all looks like a blur to me."

"You got to read the signs, son," said Sheriff Cantwell. "See here, these tracks are from horses that are shed; you can tell that there are two riders because one set of tracks is deeper than the others. That tells me that one of the men was a big man."

Andy laughed. "You mean that Lane can read sign better than you? How can that be possible?"

"His daddy taught him," explained the sheriff. "I once saw Morg trail two men more than five hundred miles and never lose the trail once. He captured both of those men and brought them in for trial."

"I don't think I'm going to be a horse thief with two guys like you and Lane around," said Andy, laughing.

"What do you suggest we do now, Josh?" asked John.

"Well, these tracks are heading west from here," said the sheriff. "Unless I miss my guess, they will turn north later."

"You mean you know where they are going?" asked Tom.

"It's only a guess, but I wouldn't be surprised if I know," said Sheriff Cantwell. "What say we head for Cal Rowan's spread. I have another hunch that we'll meet him coming this way."

126

29

Lane, along with Cal and Gil, arrived at the C-R Connected and went right to the pasture where Cal kept his horse herd. Lane immediately dismounted and looked at the telltale tracks. He kept walking back and forth over the ground. Finally he stood to his feet.

"You're right," he said. "There were two riders. One of them is a mighty big man, which gives me some clue as to who it might be."

"You mean you already know one of the men?" asked Gil.

"I'm only guessing, and that might be wrong to suspect a man when you don't have more to go on," said Lane. "Let's follow these tracks a little way."

The tracks led to the southwest for a while and then began heading toward the north.

"You had those horses branded, didn't you, Cal?" asked Lane.

"Yeah, we vented the brands the same day we bought them from you," answered Cal. "I do that with any stock I buy."

"Good idea," affirmed Lane.

They were now heading straight north when Lane stopped and said to Cal, "Let's head for the Rocking R and check with the sheriff and Mister Redfield. I'd like to compare notes with Sheriff Cantwell."

They had gone only a few miles when they saw four riders heading toward them. "There's the sheriff now," said Lane, "along with Mister Redfield—"

"You mean you can see who they are from this distance!" said Gil.

"Yeah, I can tell by the horses they're riding," said Lane.

"You sure have good eyes," commented Gil. As the riders came together, it became apparent that Lane was right.

"What did you find out, Lane?" asked Sheriff Cantwell.

"Two riders, heading north," said Lane, "one of them a very big man."

The sheriff turned to John Redfield and grinned. John nodded to him and asked, "Do you two know who did this?"

"We would only be guessing right now, but I think Lane is thinking the same thing I am," answered the sheriff.

"How about letting us in on it?" suggested Cal.

"Well, you have all heard about the fight that Lane had in town one day. The guy he fought with was named Lee Jorms, and, I'm sure you heard, Lane knocked the slop out of him. The time this same man picked the fight with Tom, I had occasion to stick a gun in his ribs. He said then that he would get even with me and, later, he did," answered Sheriff Cantwell. "I've kind of got the idea in my head that he is now getting even with Lane."

"How would that be getting even with Lane?" asked Cal. "He stole the horses from John and me, not Lane."

"I'll give you two guesses where we find them," said the sheriff. "What do you think, Lane?"

"You're ahead of me, Mister Cantwell," said Lane. "I thought they would drive them across the mountains and sell them."

"Hey, here comes a rider and he's really burning the breeze," offered Andy.

"That's Renny!" said Lane. "I wonder what's got him

so excited; he doesn't ride like that without a reason."

As the rider drew near, they saw that it, indeed, was Renny. His eyes were big as though he had a very important secret to tell.

"Lane, Mister Cantwell, you aren't going to believe this!" he blurted out, excitedly. "Lane, you know those horses you sold to Mister Rowan and Mister Redfield?"

"Want me to tell you where they are, Renny?" asked the sheriff.

"Where?" asked Renny.

"In with Lane's other horses," said the sheriff. "That's what I meant when I said I'd give you two guesses."

"That's what you meant when you said he was getting even with Lane," said John. "He would figure we would blame Lane for rustling them."

"Right as rain," said the sheriff, "and the worst part is, we can't prove he did it; nobody saw him."

"What do we do next, then?" asked Cal. "Do we just let him get away with it?"

"What else can we do?" asked Sheriff Cantwell. "If you go accusing somebody of something, you better be able to prove it."

"Renny, was that Appaloosa with Cal's other horses?" asked Lane.

"He sure was!" said Renny, still excited. "That's what made me look to see how many horses were there; I saw him first."

"Well, gentlemen, you now know where your horses are; you can get them anytime, and while you are at it, you better get Sheriff Cantwell to arrest me for rustling," said Lane, smiling.

"Hey, that's a good idea; you better put handcuffs on him, Sheriff, he looks like a desperate character to me," said Cal Rowan, laughing.

The sheriff laughed along with the rest of the men, and then said, "Lane, if I were you, I'd be mighty careful until that Jorms either leaves these parts or is captured."

"What would you arrest him for, Sheriff?" asked Lane. "You can't prove he stole those horses."

"No, you're right there, Lane, but I can get him for assaulting an officer of the law," said the sheriff.

"You're right, Sheriff, I forgot about that," said Lane. "But wouldn't you have to have a witness to prove he did that?"

"Yeah, but I could hold him for a day or two," said Sheriff Cantwell.

"Sheriff, you be awful careful if you go to arrest that guy," said Tom. "I found out the hard way that he's nobody to fool with."

"I'll cross that bridge when I come to it," said the sheriff.

The men all headed for the Slash S, which was the Streeter brand. The sheriff started back for town.

30

About two miles west of Blue Spring, Lee and Val Jorms had set up camp beside a small stream. Val was busy frying bacon over a small fire while his brother was rubbing down the horses with dried grass.

"Lee, I still think we would be wise to move on and get away from these parts," said Val. "Now that you've gotten even with that Streeter kid, there's no good reason to hang around here anymore."

"You let me worry about that," said Lee. "Besides, I want to make sure we got even with him. I don't see what else that dumb sheriff can do but throw him in jail. Those ranchers will be fit to be tied when they find their horses in with his."

"They may not even suspect him, Lee," said Val. "Anybody who can read sign can figger out what happened."

"Ah, these yo-yos around here are too dumb to know anything like that" said Lee, sneering. "But to make sure it worked, you sneak into town tonight and see what happened. If I go in, that sheriff is liable to try and arrest me; not that he could, but why stir up any more trouble right now."

When the coffee began to boil, Val got out two tin cups and plates, filled the cups, and put the bacon on their plates. Lee came over and sat down.

"Boy, that coffee tastes good," he said.

Val got some hardtack out of his saddlebags and offered some to Lee. After they had finished eating, Val cleaned their utensils and began saddling his horse. Being in no hurry, he took his time getting into town. He tied up at the hitch rail of the Lone Eagle saloon and walked inside. Gus came over and asked his pleasure.

"Whiskey," said Val. "What's new?"

Gus poured his whiskey and shrugged his shoulders. "What can be new in this town?"

"Well, you had a bank holdup and a hanging; I'd say that was something to make a person sit up and take notice," said Val.

"Yeah, but that was some time ago, now," answered Gus. "Nothing's happened lately."

Just then the door opened and Sheriff Cantwell walked in. Glancing around, he saw Val standing at the bar and walked over.

"I thought I saw you come in here," he said to Val. "I want to ask you some questions."

"Why sure, Sheriff, what's on your mind?" asked Val.

"Where's that brother of yours? I want to see him about several things," said the sheriff.

"Sheriff, I haven't seen him since that day out at Blue Spring, and you know I wasn't in on that," said Val. "That was Lee's idea."

"I know you weren't, because, if you were, you wouldn't be standing here now, you'd be in jail," said the sheriff. "You say you haven't seen your brother since then; are you sure you weren't with him a few nights ago?"

"What makes you ask that?" said Val.

"I think you know what I'm talking about, but, just in case you don't, two amateur horse thieves tried to make it look like Lane Streeter had stolen some horses from some ranchers around here," explained Sheriff Cantwell. "Lane knew immediately who one of the men was. If your brother keeps on fooling around with Lane, he's going to get hurt and hurt bad. And, if you see your brother, tell him that Cal Rowan has promised to hang anybody he

132

catches fooling around with his stock."

"I'll tell him if I see him," said Val, "but I think he's been down in Texas for about two weeks."

"Sure, sure, and I've been in Washington giving the president advice," said the sheriff, laughing. "Well, you tell him anyway."

Val finished his drink and hurried from the saloon. He got on his horse and headed out of town the opposite way he had come in. When he was well out of town, he swung around and headed for their camp. Lee wasn't in camp, so Val put some water on to heat for coffee. As the water began to boil, he heard Lee riding into camp.

"Want some coffee?" Val asked.

"Okay, that sounds good," said Lee. "What did you find out?"

"That sheriff saw me ride in and came into the saloon and asked me some questions," said Val.

"What kind of questions?" asked Lee.

"Well, first of all, your plan to get Lane Streeter in trouble failed," said Val. "That sheriff said that Streeter knew right away that you were one of the men. The sheriff suspected that I was the other one, but he can't prove it."

"How could Streeter or anyone else know that I was one of the men?" asked Lee.

"I don't know, but the sheriff called us a couple of amateurs," said Val. "You remember I told you that anyone who could read sign could figger it out. The sheriff said that Streeter knew right away who one of the men was. He didn't say how he knew. He also said to tell you that Cal Rowan said that if he caught anyone fooling with his stock, he was going to hang him."

"Well, looks like we got some paying back to do," said Lee. "That kid Streeter has been lucky so far, but his luck is about to run out."

"Look, Lee, right now we can ride out of here with no trouble," said Val. "Nobody will be on our trail. That sheriff isn't going to try and find you for beating him up, but if we hang around here and cause more trouble, we're going to find it."

"It wasn't your jaw that was broken," snorted Lee. "That kid is going to pay for that if it's the last thing I ever do. I'd still like to know how he knew I was in on stealing those horses. You didn't admit to it, did you?"

"No, I lied to the sheriff and told him I hadn't seen you for several weeks, and that I didn't know where you are now. He didn't believe me; he thinks I was with you in taking those horses," said Val.

"I know one way to get back at him," said Lee, gloatingly. "That little filly I tried to kiss in town that day; he's sweet on her. Besides, I wouldn't mind seeing her again. She kind of took my eye."

"You aren't figgering to hurt her in any way, are you?" asked Val. "I don't want any part of something like that."

"You let me handle that part of it," said Lee. "If I persuade her to ride off with us, he'll follow, sure as I'm a foot high."

"Lee, that's kidnapping!" exclaimed Val. "Are you trying to get us hung?"

"Don't worry, I know what I'm doing," said Lee. "I'll just take a ride over there first thing in the morning."

"Sorry, Lee, I don't agree with what you're doing," said Val. "I won't be going with you."

"That's okay, I don't want you along," said Lee.

31

Bob Holiday was in the barn loading his buckboard with vegetables. This was the busy time of the year, with all the vegetables and fruit ripening. He and his wife, Jennie, had done well this year, with just the right amount of rain. He glanced out the door and saw his daughter Elaine hurrying out to the wash that she had hung out earlier. He realized that a few drops of rain were beginning to fall, and he saw why she was hurrying. He was proud of this very beautiful daughter of his. He was also proud of her choice of men, for he had long been an admirer of Lane Streeter. He and Morg had been close friends.

He suddenly realized that a horse was approaching. Looking out, he saw the man who had annoyed his daughter in town, and he wondered what he could want, coming here. He walked over to the corner where he kept a shotgun fully loaded.

Lee Jorms rode up to the farm and immediately saw Elaine gathering in her washing. He rode over to her. "Get up behind me, little girl, we're going for a ride," he said.

"I'm not going anywhere with you!" she retorted.

"Look, you heard me the first time!" he snarled. "Don't make—"

A voice behind him cut him off short. "Mister, I don't know what you think you're doing here, but you're not wanted. No, don't try to turn around; I've got a shotgun on you, and either you turn that bronc around and ride out, or I'll blow a hole in you so big you can drive a team through it!"

"Old man, you just signed your death warrant!" snarled Jorms. "I'll catch you in—"

135

"Yeah, yeah, but that will be then, and this is now!" retorted Bob. "Mister, I'm not telling you again! Get lost, and fast!"

Jorms started to say something else when suddenly the shotgun went off with a deafening blast. Bob had purposely lowered the muzzle so as not to hit Jorms, but some of the pellets bounced up and hit the horse's legs. With a snort, the horse leaped forward and took off running. Jorms, although furious, let the horse go, knowing the danger of that other barrel.

"You wait, Mister, there's another round coming, and it will be mine!" he muttered to himself.

"Dad, he was trying to force me to go with him," said Elaine.

"I think we had better inform the sheriff about this. And it won't hurt to let Lane know," said Bob. "Well, from now on, this shotgun goes with me until this thing is settled. There's no telling what that guy will try next."

The sprinkle had stopped, but Elaine finished taking down the clothes and took them into the house. Her mother had come to the door when the shotgun had gone off, and she asked Elaine what had happened. Elaine explained what had taken place.

"What's the matter with that man? Is he crazy, or what?" asked Jennie.

"I don't know, but I do know that he scares me half to death," said Elaine.

"Do you think it's safe for your father to go into town?" asked Jennie.

"I don't know, I hadn't thought about that," admitted Elaine. "Maybe we should go with him."

"He would never hear to that," said Jennie.

"We could tell him we want to do some shopping," suggested Elaine.

"That's an idea," said Jennie. "Maybe if we were with him, that awful man would think twice about causing any trouble."

"Mom, that man is horrible; nothing would stop him, he has no scruples at all," said Elaine.

Just then Bob came in from the barn and announced that he was leaving for town. "We're going with you, Bob," said Jennie. "We want to do some shopping."

"Well, all right, but I'm going to be there for some time," said Bob.

When they arrived in town, Bob went into the store with Jennie and Elaine, for Ed Danvers was one of his best customers. After unloading nearly half of his load with Ed, he headed next for the sheriff's office. Sheriff Cantwell was seated in his usual place, outside the office door. Bob informed him of what had taken place.

"Seems that fellow is bent on building up more trouble for himself," commented the sheriff. "I don't suppose you know where he went, do you?"

"No, I don't have any idea," said Bob. "But you better be sure of one thing; this shotgun goes with me wherever I go. That guy told me I had signed my death warrant when I held that shotgun on him."

The sheriff looked up and saw Lane Streeter riding by. He hailed him and waved him over to the office.

"Hi, Sheriff; hi, Mister Holiday, what's new?" asked Lane.

The sheriff informed him of what had taken place out at the Holiday farm. Lane scowled and said, "Some folks never learn, do they? Any idea where that goofball might be?"

"No idea," said Sheriff Cantwell, "but his brother was in town last night and denies even seeing him. I think he was lying, but I can't prove it."

"I wouldn't believe either of them if they swore on a stack of Bibles," said Lane. "Mister Holiday, if I were you, I wouldn't let Elaine go riding anywhere until this guy is put away."

"She hasn't been—and won't be," assured Bob. "From now on wherever I go, this goes with me," he said, holding up the shotgun. "Well, I got work to do."

"Mister Cantwell, can you jail him on that kidnapping threat?" asked Lane.

"He would only lie out of it," said the sheriff. "But I can get him for assault, and I will if I see him."

"Better have your gun out when you go to arrest him," suggested Lane.

"I intend to," said the sheriff. "Don't forget, he threatened you, too."

"I'm looking forward to meeting him again," said Lane, "and you better believe I'll be careful. Well, be seeing you, Sheriff."

Lane turned Midnight and cantered down to Danvers Store. Elaine saw him coming and stepped out to meet him.

"I heard what happened, honey, and I want you to promise me you'll be careful, and don't go riding out by yourself until that guy's hash is settled," said Lane.

"I'm not about to, Lane," she said. "That man gives me the shivers whenever I even think of him."

"Well, that's a load off my mind," said Lane. "The sheriff is going to throw him in jail whenever he sees him," he said, trying to ease her mind.

Nobody was watching, so he took her in his arms and kissed her.

"Lane, someone will see us!" she said, red-faced.

"Let 'em," he said, grinning. "Tell you what, let's meet in town on Saturday. Renny and I are selling some more horses, and I'll treat us all to dinner. That means your folks, too. Of course, Mom and Callie will be there, along with Renny and his mom."

"Sounds great to me," said Elaine. "I'll tell Dad and Mom on the way home."

"Fine, see you on Saturday then," Lane said, and, before she could resist, he kissed her again.

32

"It's no use talking any more about it: I've made up my mind," said Lee Jorms. He and his brother were having an argument.

"Lee, all you're going to do is get yourself killed!" said Val. "Do you realize that if you had kidnapped that girl, this whole area would have been after your scalp?"

"Bah, there's nothing to that! Look how I handled that sheriff," said Lee. "Val, you've never hated the way I do. First, it was the old man kicking us around the way he did until we had to run away from home. Well, I got him, didn't I? It took a while, but after I grew up, I went back and settled his hash. After that, I made up my mind that nobody is going to cross me without paying for it."

"But, Lee, this is different; these people around here haven't done anything to you that you didn't ask for," said Val. "How can you hate them for that?"

"Mighty easy, Val," said Lee. "What about you? What were you after when he knocked you silly? Wasn't that just as wrong?"

"Yeah, but I don't hate him for it," said Val. "We were planning to steal more of his horses and sell them. We left our horses there and took three of his. Gib passed himself off as a U.S. marshal to just get the lay of the land. We were going to go back later and steal about fifty more. That kid, Streeter, got the sheriff and corralled us in town. Gib went to belt him and Streeter kind of manhandled him. We aimed to get even for that and that kid whipped all three of us. Lee, I don't hate him for that; he was just protecting himself."

"Well, I hate his guts!" said Lee, passionately. "And

I'm going to get even if I have to kill him to do it!"

"Well, that's where you and I are different," said Val. "But, Lee, leave that girl alone; she will only get you in more trouble."

"I'll do whatever I have to," said Lee, "anything to lure him into a trap."

"Well, I'm riding on then, Lee," said Val. "Take care of yourself."

"Sure, kid," said Lee.

Val saddled up and rode off toward the west. Lee began preparations for supper.

In the meantime, Lane rode into Haleyville to make preparations for Saturday. He went into the dining room and found Aunt Abby sprucing up the place. He informed her of his plans. "How many will be here?" she asked.

"Nine, all told," he said. "And we'll be in for dinner about five o'clock."

"Everything will be ready," Abby promised, smiling. "I'll even see if I can't find some arsenic for your food."

"Good, I'm glad everything will be normal, then," he said, laughing.

33

Lane had found out that Saturday was Renny's birthday. He conspired with his mother to fix up a card for Renny. She didn't know what he had in mind. She got some paper and folded it to look like a card. She decorated the edges with red paint and drew hearts on it. Lane was well pleased with her efforts.

"I'll take over from here, Mom," he said. Unknown to her, he penciled in the words *Love and Kisses,* and signed it *All My Love, Callie.*

That afternoon, all the parties were gathered in the large dining room. Abby had decorated the room in a beautiful fashion. Streamers hung from the lighting fixtures. Many other diners were there also, thus the room was nearly filled. The usual jocularity went on between Lane and Abby, and everyone was having a wonderful time. After the main meal was eaten and everyone was filled to repletion, Abby came in carrying a birthday cake with the letters RENNY. Lane had managed to have Callie seated next to Renny. Renny was dumbfounded. He wasn't used to being the center of attention; his face was very red. He had to blow out the candles that Abby had placed on the cake. After he did so, Lane handed, him an envelope.

"Someone told me to give this to you," he said, grinning.

Renny took the envelope from him and muttered, "You folks shouldn't have done this."

"Open it and show us what it says," said his mother. Renny seemed to be all thumbs. After what seemed a long time, he finally got it open and withdrew the contents. As he read it, his face was suffused with color. He was too embarrassed to speak. Sheriff Cantwell, who was one of the guests, spoke up.

"What's the matter, son, the cat got your tongue?" he asked.

Finally Renny blurted out, "Gee, thanks, Callie!"

"What? What's that supposed to mean?" asked Callie.

"Oh, oh, I smell a rat," said Martha. "May I see that, please?"

Renny silently handed the card to her. Martha took it and read the contents. She looked accusingly at Lane, but before she could speak, she burst into laughter.

"What's so funny, Mom?" asked Callie.

Martha handed the card to her. She took it and began to read. Suddenly her face, too, was suffused with red.

"Lane Streeter, so help me, I'm going to shoot you the first chance I get!" she blurted out.

"You mean he's the one who wrote that?" asked Renny. To show he could take a joke, he then said, "Now I'm disappointed."

Martha, to let everyone in on it, took the card and read it aloud. Everyone burst into laughter. Callie also had to laugh. Sheriff Cantwell, to cover the embarrassment both Callie and Renny felt, said, "Well, son, it's not every day that a fellow becomes sixteen; congratulations, Renny."

"Thank you, Sir," he said. "And thank all you wonderful people, even Lane."

They all laughed anew at this quip. Sheriff Cantwell stood up and said, "Thank you all for inviting me. I would have hated to miss this party, especially Renny's card. Now I have to get back to the office."

This seemed to be the cue for the party to end. They

143

all stood up and began to leave. Lane got Abby aside and handed her a check. "Thanks for everything, Aunt Abby," he said. "I have to admit, the food was great."

"Thank you, Lane, I enjoyed doing it for you," she said. "That little touch of humor only added to the occasion."

He grinned and said, "I'll never forget that look on Renny's face if I live to be a million years old."

They all sauntered out to the street where they stood talking. Martha, Jennie, and Callie were in one group, while the sheriff, Bob, Renny, and his mother were talking about Renny's future.

"What do you plan to do, son?" asked Sheriff Cantwell.

"Well, right now I just like working for Lane; he is really good to me," said Renny. "I was hoping I could stay in school, but Dad's death changed all that. Mom and I are saving our money hoping to buy a few cattle and make a go of it that way."

Elaine and Lane were off to one side enjoying each other's company. "Lane, that's awful the way you tease Callie and Renny," she said, and then, chuckling, she added, "I'll never forget the look on Callie's face when she read what you wrote."

Lane grinned. "I'll probably find thistles in my bed sometime soon. She will get even one way or another."

Suddenly along the street came the pounding of a horse's hooves. Lee Jorms swept along toward them, his face contorted with rage, his pistol drawn. As he got near, he fired toward Lane. Firing a gun from a galloping horse is very uncertain. He fired the second time and galloped on past. There was a piercing scream from Martha. The bullet had struck Callie and she dropped to the ground, unconscious. Hearing the scream, Lane turned and ran toward Callie. Blood was streaming from a wound in her chest. Dropping on his knees, he gathered her up in his arms.

"Someone get Doc Baldwin!" he yelled. He went up the steps of the hotel and into the dining room. Abby, hearing the shots, had started out to investigate.

"Lane, what's wrong?" she asked.

With tears streaming down his face, Lane said, "That guy Jorms shot Callie and I know she's hurt—"

"Bring her in here," Abby interrupted, leading the way to her bedroom. "Lay her here on my bed."

By this time, Martha was right behind them. Though crying, she had gained control of herself. "Doc will probably need hot water and a wash rag," she ventured.

Abby hastened to get the necessary items. Just then, Doc Baldwin burst into the room. Seeing Callie lying on the bed, he immediately went to work.

"Lane, clear the room! Martha, you and Abby may stay; everybody else, out," he ordered.

"How bad is she, Doc?" begged Lane, imploringly.

"I don't know yet, Lane," said Doc, gently. "As soon as I know anything, I'll let you know."

Lane left the room, only to bump into Renny, who was openly crying. "Lane, is she—?"

"Doc doesn't know anything yet, Renny," he said. "He wants us to wait outside."

"Lane, I never wanted to kill anybody before, but now I do!" Renny blurted out.

"That makes two of us!" said Lane vehemently.

They went back out to the street where a crowd had now gathered. Elaine immediately came over to Lane. He put his head on her shoulder and wept openly.

"I didn't come in because I was afraid I would just clutter up the place," she explained.

145

"You were right, honey," he managed to say. "Doc cleared the room right away."

Just then, Reverend Manning came up to Lane. "Lane, I just heard what happened. Is there anything I can do?" he asked. "If so, just name it."

"Doc says that all we can do is wait," Lane said. "Thank you for coming."

"It's the least I could do," said Reverend Manning. "I know this has to be hard on you and your mother also. This is the time to lean on God and his promises."

"Reverend Manning, there's one thing I want to do right now," said Lane, "and that's to get my hands on that Jorms guy!"

"I can understand your feeling that way," said Reverend Manning, "but right now that wouldn't be best for you."

Sheriff Cantwell came riding up on his horse. Seeing Lane, he veered over to talk to him. "Lane, I'm starting after Jorms. I may be able to track him down, for his horse will leave deeper prints than ordinary," he said.

"I'm going home and get Midnight," said Lane. "I came in with Mom and Callie in the buggy. I didn't even have my gun with me."

"Son, let me give you some advice; let me go after this guy," said the sheriff. "Right now, your mother needs you more than anything."

"The sheriff is right, Lane," Reverend Manning said, gently.

"Okay, I'll stay here; you are both right," said Lane. Turning, he went back up the steps into the dining room. He sat at one of the tables and lowered his head in his arms. Thoughts raced wildly through his head. If he only had her back, he wouldn't tease her so much.

"Oh, Callie, please get well," he sobbed. He felt an

arm on his shoulders. He looked up to see Elaine there with him. Behind her stood Reverend Manning.

"Lane, let's allow Reverend Manning to have prayer with us," said Elaine. "Isn't that why we go to church?"

"You're right, of course," said Lane, and he silently bowed his head.

"Lord, you tell us in your word that you're a friend that sticketh closer than a brother," began Reverend Manning. "You also tell us that if we ask anything in your name, you will do it. Well, Lord, we're asking now. We need your help. We are so human. Lord, you know Callie is such an innocent little girl. She had no part in what went on. Yet, here she is, the victim of an evil man's desire to maim and kill. Lord, you healed so many people when you walked this earth; we ask you to perform another miracle. Lord, heal Lane's and Martha's hearts. Give them the calmness that can come only from you. And, Lord, heal Callie's body. These things are so difficult for us as humans, but for you, they are as nothing. We ask these things in your name. Amen."

Lane was amazed, for as Reverend Manning was praying, a strange calmness seemed to steal over him. "Thank you, Reverend Manning, your being here means so much," he said. "And thank you, honey, for thinking of prayer."

Suddenly Martha appeared in the doorway. She came over to them.

"Mom, is there any news yet?" asked Lane.

"No, but the doctor says she's hurt very bad," said Martha, the grief showing in her eyes.

"Martha, if there's anything you want me to do, all you have to do is ask," said Reverend Manning.

"Thank you, Reverend Manning," she said. "The only thing I can think of is prayer. Lane, I'm going to stay here

147

all night. Doc says Callie can't be moved, and Abby told me to stay if I want to."

"All right, Mom," said Lane. "I'm going to go home and do the chores and come back. I want to get Midnight in case I have to go after Jorms."

"Son, I don't want you going after him; I would rather you stayed around close," said Martha.

"I'll be right where you want me, Mom," he said. "I'll be back in a little while."

Just as Lane was leaving, Doc Baldwin came into the dining room.

"Doc, is she—?"

"No, Lane, she's okay for right now; I just wanted to let you in on what I know," said Doc. "I'll not lie to you; she's badly hurt. I don't know if she's going to make it or not. A forty-five slug is an awesome thing to get hit with, and Callie is a little girl. The bullet hit her in the upper part of her chest on the left side. There is a huge hole where the bullet came out the back. She has lost a lot of blood. She is still unconscious. When will she come to? I don't know. When can she be moved? I don't know. What are her chances? Very slim. We should know better in a few days. I'm sorry to be so brutally frank, but I want to be honest with you. Any questions?"

"Thank you, Doc, for being so honest," said Martha. "We would rather know how serious it is, rather than have you give us false hope."

"I'll be staying here all night to keep an eye on her," said Doc.

"Thank you again, Doc," said Lane. "I'll be here also if there is anything I can do."

34

When Lane got back from the ranch, he was surprised to find Renny in the dining room.

"After I took Mom home, I wanted to come back here and stay," he said. "Aunt Abby said we could stay in here if we wanted to."

"Thanks for wanting to stay," said Lane. "This all seems like a nightmare to me."

"Yeah, me too," said Renny.

As the hours went by, the tension seemed to mount. Lane found himself getting more anxious. Occasionally, Martha would come out and sit with him. Renny was openly crying. Martha tried to comfort him.

"She's just got to get well, Mrs. Streeter!" he blurted out. "God won't let anything happen to her, will He?"

"We know He's looking after her now," she said. "Whether it's His will for her to get well, we don't know. We can only pray."

Sheriff Cantwell stepped softly into the room. He came over to Martha and Lane. "How's she doing?" he asked.

"Doc says she's still hanging on, Sheriff," said Martha.

"Good for her," said the sheriff. "Lane, I tracked him for quite a ways; I finally lost his trail well out past Blue Spring. He took to the rocks then and I lost him."

"Sheriff, if it takes the rest of my life, I'll find him," said Lane. "I can't leave here now, but when this is over, I'll get him."

"I know how you feel, son, and I can't say as I blame you," said Sheriff Cantwell. "There may be some things in our favor. He might not know he shot Callie, and thus may hang around these parts, hoping to get another crack at you."

"I never thought of that, Sheriff," said Lane, "but that makes sense."

Abby appeared with a tray of sandwiches and coffee. "Maybe this will help lift your spirits a little," she said.

"Thank you, Abby," said Martha. "Right now I couldn't eat a thing, but that coffee will help."

The sheriff drank some coffee and got up to leave. "I'll be in the office if you need me, Lane."

Martha went back in to be with Callie. Time seemed to drag by. It was getting near midnight when Renny finally dozed off. Lane's mind was filled with emotions. Abby came out with more coffee.

"Is there anything else you need, Lane?" she asked.

"Aunt Abby, this is the toughest thing I have ever faced in my life," he said. "Now I wish I hadn't teased her so much. Remember what you told me years ago?"

"What was that, Lane?" she asked.

"Back when Dad was killed, you helped me so much," he said. "You said then that we would cry in the tomorrows of our life; well, that tomorrow is here and I'm crying plenty. Now I feel so sorry that I pulled that joke on her and Renny."

"No, no, Lane, you mustn't feel that way!" Abby exclaimed. "Those are some of the good moments of our lives. She enjoyed those times the same as all of us do."

"Oh, Aunt Abby, if I could only be sure of that!" Lane exclaimed.

"Let me ask you a question," said Abby. "Did you ever tease that man who shot her?"

"Are you kidding?" Lane asked. "I wouldn't tease him about anything!"

"Exactly!" said Abby. "Don't you see, Lane? We only tease the ones we love and care for the most. That is what life is all about: caring and loving. That's why this hurts so much. You love her so much. Lane, I wish I could tell you that Callie is going to get well, but I can't. Those things we just have to commit to God."

"Aunt Abby, you are good for me," said Lane. "You seem to know how to straighten me out when I need it the most. Now, I feel better."

"Well, I'm glad. Now, why don't you try to get some sleep?" she asked.

"Aunt Abby, I couldn't sleep now if I had to," he said. "This just keeps going through my mind. Sometimes I wish I could wake up and find out this is all a horrible nightmare."

"That's only natural, but that isn't the way life really is," she said. "We have to live it the way it is."

"Yeah, I'm finding out," Lane said.

"And do you know what?" Abby asked. "You'll be a better person because of it. God uses these life experiences to temper us. Then it all depends on the way we respond. If we see it in the right way, we are better prepared to meet whatever comes our way."

"That's as good a sermon as I've ever preached," spoke up a voice from the doorway. They looked up to see Reverend Manning standing there. "Abby, that is good preaching in any language."

"I didn't mean it that way," Abby hesitatingly explained.

"Truth is truth, no matter who says it," said Reverend Manning. "And if I ever heard the truth, it was now."

"What are you doing here, Reverend Manning?" asked Lane. "You have a sermon to preach tomorrow."

"I wanted to spend time with you in your time of need,

Lane," said Reverend Manning. "What kind of minister would I be if I neglected my duty?"

"Well, I'll go in the kitchen now; call me if you need me, Lane," Abby said.

"Thank you, Aunt Abby," said Lane.

35

In his camp just east of Blue Spring, Val Jorms was preparing supper. He was frying bacon, and the smell was tantalizing. He got some hardtack out of his saddlebags and a tin cup. The coffee was boiling, and that, too, had a good aroma. He was thoroughly enjoying his meal and his mind went back to Lee. He hadn't heard anything from him and he wondered what he had been up to. He finished his meal and decided to go into town to see what he could find out. He quickly washed up the dishes he had used and saddled up.

"I know I shouldn't worry about him, but I do," he mused audibly to himself as he rode along. When he reached town, he tied up at the Lone Eagle and went inside. The place was empty except for Gus.

"Where is everybody?" Val asked.

"Hey, ain't you that Jorms guy's brother?" asked Gus.

"Yeah, why do you want to know?" asked Val.

"It might not be too safe for you after what happened," said Gus.

"What do you mean, after what happened?" he asked.

"You mean you don't know? Your brother came through town and tried to shoot Lane Streeter," said Gus. "He missed Lane, but one of the bullets hit Lane's little sister, Callie. They don't expect her to live."

"Oh, no, not that!" moaned Val. "What got into him, I wonder?"

"Haven't you seen him?" asked Gus.

"No, I really haven't," said Val. "He told me he had

some idea of getting even with Streeter. I couldn't go along with that, so we kind of split up."

"If he comes back here, the people will probably hang him," said Gus.

"Where is the kid he shot?" asked Val. "I suppose she would be at the doctor's office."

"No, Doc Baldwin said it's too dangerous to move her; she's at the hotel," said Gus.

"Well, I sure hope she gets well. I'll be riding, for you could be right; people might think I had something to do with it," said Val. "Is the sheriff at his office?"

"No, he's out looking for your brother," said Gus.

"If you see him, tell him I had nothing to do with it," said Val. "I'm against anything like that. I'm not claiming to be an angel or anything like that, but what Lee did was wrong."

"Okay, I'll do that," said Gus.

It was late when Val got back to his camp. He built up the fire and heated the coffee.

"Well, Lee, you've gone and done it now," he mused aloud. "You'll never be able to go back to that town again."

*   *   *

Lee Jorms was angry with himself. He was sure he had that kid in his sights, and yet he had missed him. *Well, there's a next time coming, kid,* he thought. *And the next time, I won't miss.*

He didn't realize what he had done. He thought the scream had been some woman who was scared. He figured that he had better lay low for a while. He didn't know if anybody was following him or not. At first, he headed for Blue Spring, but realizing that Sheriff Cantwell might

154

suspect that, he turned and rode north. It was getting late when he pulled up to the hideout. He lit the lamps that Brady Hatch had used. The table was thick with dust. He went outside and gathered some kindling. After he got a fire started, he took inventory of the food supply. There were some potatoes that were beginning to sprout, and some onions that were beginning to show age. He found a slab of bacon and with the coffee he had in his saddle-bags; he figured that would hold him.

While he was eating, he began wondering what he should do next. He wondered where Val was. That fool kid was too soft; he couldn't see that anything you wanted, you took. If somebody gets in your way, you bump him off. That Streeter kid might have won one round, but the game wasn't over yet. Another thought came to him: that girl's old man had stuck a shotgun in his ribs. He would pay for that. Why not get the Streeter kid first, then that Holiday and, while he was at it, take the girl with him? With these ideas in mind, he turned in and slept.

36

This had been the longest night that Lane Streeter could ever remember. With the coming of daylight, he rose from the chair in which he had been sitting and stretched. Doc Baldwin came into the dining room.

"Well, she's still with us, son," he said. "A couple of times I was afraid we had lost her, but she rallied."

"How long before you know anything definite, Doc?" asked Lane.

"I really can't say for sure," the doctor replied. "Once she gets over the shock, she will begin to improve."

"What you're saying is that you don't know if she will get over the shock, is that it?" asked Lane.

"That's it all right, Lane," said Doc. "I wish I could make it easier for you, but I can't."

Just then Martha appeared in the doorway. She was haggard and drawn. Suddenly she burst into tears. Lane went over and took her in his arms.

"Lane, I'm terribly scared. She just lies there, so helpless, and I can't do anything for her," said Martha, sobbing.

"Mom, that's two of us who are scared," said Lane. "If I could only take her place, I'd do it gladly."

Doc came over and put his arms around both of them. "Now hold on here a minute," he said. "She isn't dead yet and she just might pull through this. One thing I didn't tell you because I didn't want to build up any false hopes; her pulse is a little stronger this morning. Now, that's a small thing, but it is encouraging."

"Thank you, Doc," said Martha. "I don't know what we would do without you."

Abby came into the dining room and announced, "Anyone wanting to get washed up for breakfast had better do so now, for it will be ready in a few minutes."

"I'm not a mind reader, but I know what you were going to say, Martha," said Doc, "but you have to eat to keep up your strength."

"Did someone mention food?" asked Renny, raising his head from the table where he had spent the night.

"Renny, I thought you had gone home," said Martha.

"I did, but I came back. How is she, Doc?" he asked.

"We don't know yet, son, but she's holding her own," said Doc.

Bob Holiday, along with his family, walked into the room. Elaine went over to Lane and asked, "How is she, Lane? Is she going to be all right?"

"We don't know yet, honey, but Doc says she's holding her own," he said. "Did you come in for church?"

"I came in to be with you," she answered. "Reverend Manning will have to get along without me today."

"He was here all night," said Lane. "He just left about an hour ago."

"Doc, is it all right if Elaine and I look in on Callie?" asked Lane. "We promise not to stay."

"Sure, it will be okay; just don't try to talk to her," admonished Doc.

They stepped quietly into the room where Callie lay. She looked so small and frail that Lane was shocked. He wanted to tell her to get up and be okay again. A sob escaped him. Elaine gently squeezed his arm. He raised his head toward heaven and silently prayed, "Lord, please let her live."

On an inspiration, he went out and motioned to Renny. Renny came over to him and asked, "What is it, Lane?"

Lane took him by the arm and drew him into Callie's room. Renny stood looking at her for a moment and silently began to cry. Martha took him in her arms, trying to comfort him. They walked out of the room; Renny couldn't talk. Finally, he was able to say, "Thanks for allowing me to see her."

John Redfield appeared in the doorway. He came over to them and quietly put his arm around Martha. "How is she?" he asked.

Doc, seeing Martha was having trouble speaking, gave John the information on Callie.

John turned to Lane and said, "Son, Tom and Andy are out at your place looking after things. If there's anything else you need, just let me know."

"That's very kind of you, Mister Redfield," said Lane. "We really appreciate it."

"Think nothing of it," said John. "Have you heard any more from that Jorms character?"

"No, Sheriff Cantwell trailed him for a ways, but finally lost his trail," said Lane.

"Well, it would pay to keep your eyes open," said John.

The rest of the day seemed to drag by. There was no change in Callie's condition. Martha refused to leave the hotel until some definite change took place. Lane went out home for a change of clothing and brought back some things Martha had requested. Lane could see that his mother was under a severe strain. Abby, noticing this, wisely asked for her help in baking some pies. As Martha worked, the lines in her face began to soften and relax. Doc, knowing what Abby had in mind, smiled. He went back in to change the bandages on Callie. Lane told Renny it would be okay for him to go home and get some rest. He promised to get word to him if there was any change.

Sheriff Cantwell came in and informed him about Val Jorms being at the Lone Eagle and what he had said concerning his brother.

"Do you believe him?" asked Lane.

"I don't know what to think," answered the sheriff. "He may be telling the truth, or he may be lying to make it look like his own skirts are clean."

37

Four long, wearisome days went by. At times, Lane thought he would lose his mind. Martha became a hollow shell of herself. Friends were constantly dropping in to offer support and sympathy. Renny practically lived in the dining room. Sheriff Cantwell came in every day to see how Callie was doing. Reverend Manning was there to offer what support he could. Abby and John Mason kept serving meals and steadfastly refusing to take a penny for them. On the sixth day after the shooting, Doc Baldwin came out of Callie's room all smiles.

"Martha, Lane, she's awake and asking for you," he said. "Now don't go in and get her all worked up. She's not out of the woods yet, but she's well on the way."

Martha breathed a long sigh of relief and began to cry. Lane had difficulty keeping the tears from his eyes.

"Thank God," he quietly muttered. He and Martha went into Callie's room. She was very drawn and peaked, but she was smiling. "Mom, what am I doing here, and where am I?" she asked.

"Honey, you're in Aunt Abby's room; you were hurt, but you're going to be all right now," said Martha.

Lane couldn't talk. He silently squeezed her hand and walked out of the room. He sat down at a table, lowered his head in his arms and wept.

"Mom, what's the matter with Lane?" asked Callie. "He looked like he was crying."

"We both are, honey, we're just so happy you are getting well," said Martha.

Just then, Doc entered the room. "I think that had better do it for now," he said. "You can come in later. Right now, this little girl has to rest."

"We'll see you later, honey," Martha said.

She went into the dining room. Lane stood up and took her into his arms. She completely let go then, and sobbed out her thankfulness. Renny, too, was openly crying. Abby joined them and said, "You two have been through a literal hell, but now it's beginning to turn the other way."

"This is the longest week I've ever spent," said Lane, "and I don't care if I never have another one like it."

Doc came out of Callie's room. "Well, there's no infection. That wound is as clean as a whistle."

"How soon can we move her out home, Doc?" asked Lane.

"Not for quite a while," said Doc. "Let's not try to rush things at this stage of the game. She's got a long way to go."

"Okay, Doc, you're the boss," said Lane. "We'll do whatever you say."

"Well, now that I can breathe again, it's time to go back to work," said Renny. "Lane, do you want me to work on those broncs today?"

"No, Renny, tomorrow is soon enough to get back in the swing of things," said Lane. "We'll just celebrate today."

"Okay, I'll see you tomorrow then," said Renny. "Mom will sure be glad to hear about Callie."

Renny had no sooner left than Elaine walked into the dining room. Seeing the look on Lane's face, she exclaimed, "Callie's going to be okay?"

Lane grabbed her and whirled her around the room. "She sure is, honey; she regained consciousness this morning."

"Oh, thank God, Lane, I'm so happy for you, and you

161

too, Mrs. Streeter," she said.

"Thank you, Elaine," said Martha. "Now, I guess we can start getting back to normal."

"Aunt Abby, fix us up the best meal you've ever cooked," said Lane. "Only this one I'm paying for."

"Lane, that's a good idea," said Martha. "I think I can eat again, without choking on the food."

"Mom, Aunt Abby's used to us choking on her food," said Lane, grinning.

"Oh, Lane, that isn't what I meant!" said Martha.

"Let him rave, Martha, you don't know how good that sounds to me," said Abby.

"Doc, this includes you also," said Lane. "I'll check with you later and pay you what we owe you."

"Well, I don't know if I can eat. I'm that worried about your bill," said Doc, his eyes twinkling.

38

Lane and Renny had caught some more wild horses, and Lane was working with them when Renny cautioned him, "Rider coming, Lane."

Lane looked and saw the rider up the lane. "That's Val Jorms. What could he be wanting, coming here?"

Val pulled his bronc up to where Lane and Renny were working. "Okay to get down?" he asked. "I don't mean you any harm."

Lane nodded. Val dismounted and came over and halted in front of Lane.

"Streeter, I just wanted to clear up some things," he said. "First of all, I had nothing to do with what happened in town, with your sister getting shot, and all."

"Okay, I'm glad to hear that," said Lane. "But there's more than that on your mind."

"You're right, there is," said Val. "What Lee did was wrong and I'm totally against it. I'm glad your sister is going to be all right. Next, I haven't seen Lee for some time now; I don't know where he is. We split up, some time back."

"Why was that?" asked Lane.

"I just couldn't stomach what he was planning on doing," said Val.

"And what was that?" asked Lane.

"To get even with you for breaking his jaw," said Val. "Look, Streeter, I'm not claiming to be your friend, or anything like that, but I will not be a party to murder. That is what he threatened to do. I guess you don't need any convincing, after what he tried in town."

"No, you're right there," said Lane. "But I'm a little

confused. Why are you warning me?"

"Because I know Lee better than you do," said Val. "I don't want anybody killed. Lee won't stop until he figgers he's even with you, even if it means killing you. Another thing; I wasn't in favor of his beating that sheriff the way he did."

"Well, thank you for coming and telling me this," said Lane. "It sure does clear the air between us. If there's no hard feelings on your part, there certainly isn't on mine, and I'll shake on that."

Lane held out his hand, and Val did likewise. They shook hands and Val mounted up and got ready to ride off. "Remember what I told you; be on guard at all times."

As he rode off down the lane, Renny spoke up. "Wow, what do you make of that?"

"I don't really know yet," said Lane. "Only time will tell."

"If he really meant what he said, it was darned decent of him to come and tell you," said Renny.

*   *   *

It was one month to the day when Doc gave the okay for Callie to be moved back home. Lane and Martha drove in to get her. Lane took a mattress off one of the beds to make a soft ride for her. Martha also put in a pillow for Callie and a chair for herself. When they arrived at the hotel, Doc was waiting for them with eager anticipation, for he was justifiably proud of the job that he had done for Callie.

"Folks," he said to them, "I'm going to be honest with you; I never thought she would get well. I'm so happy for you."

"Doc, we will forever be in your debt," said Lane.

"Now tell us what we owe you, and we will get this little girl home."

"Now, Lane, you don't have to pay this all at once," said Doc. "You can stretch it out as long as you want."

"No, Doc, we have it and we want to pay it and get it out of the way," said Lane.

"Well, I guess about forty dollars would cover it," said Doc.

"That's just about what I figured you would say," said Lane. "But you're not getting away with it this time."

Lane wrote a check for one hundred dollars and handed it to Doc. Doc immediately began to protest, but Lane hushed him up. "Look, Doc, I happen to know that you were going to write off what Renny Barker's mother owed you concerning Mister Barker's death," said Lane. "Well, you know and I know that Callie's bill was a lot more than forty dollars, so we'll just let it go at that."

"Well, thank you, Lane," said Doc.

Lane walked into Callie's room. She was all bright-eyed with anticipation. "Are you ready to go home, Twerp?" he asked. "Or would you want to stay here a while longer?"

"Are you kidding?" she asked. "Let's go home now!"

Abby wiped a tear from her eye. "It's going to be lonely around here," she said. "Callie, it's been a pleasure having you with us."

"Aunt Abby, I never knew how much I loved you until now," said Callie. "Thank you for putting up with me."

Lane bent down and picked her up. A feeling came over him that he had never experienced before. A deep thankfulness welled up within him. "Little Sister, you don't know what this day means to me," he said. "I never realized how much I loved you until you were hurt. Honey, you will never know how thankful I am for this day."

Callie, looking up, saw that his eyes were moist, and she then realized how much he really cared. "Aunt Abby's been telling me how lucky I am to have a brother like you," she said. "And, Lane, I'm so glad to be going home again. I can't remember all that happened, but Aunt Abby says I'm lucky to be alive."

"You had us worried for a while there, but everything's okay again now," Lane said, and, grinning, added, "Renny's been kind of worried, too."

Callie giggled and said, "I'm glad he's worried, so how do you like that?"

"Just fine, Little Partner. Well, here's the wagon; now let's get you comfortable," he said. He gently laid her on the mattress. Martha pulled a blanket up over her.

"How's that, honey?" she asked.

"I feel fine, Mom," Callie said.

As Lane took the reins, he noticed that practically the whole town was there to wish Callie well. Reverend Manning summed it up for them as he said, "God bless you, Callie; we love you."

On the way home, Lane drove slowly so as not to make the ride too bumpy. Many thoughts raced through his mind. Where was Jorms? Would he leave the area now? Did he even know what he had done? All questions and no answers. He knew in time the answers would come. He knew that he would have to be alert, for there was no way that he could predict Jorms's actions. He tried to analyze his own feelings toward Jorms, and found that he didn't know where to begin. Jorms had to be stopped, that much was clear. He tried to apply what he had heard Reverend Manning say many times, that we are to love everybody.

How do you love a person when that person almost kills your sister? he thought to himself. *I sure can't.*

166

39

Two weeks passed, and Callie was mending rapidly. The work for Lane and Renny had increased, for they had many orders to fill. Lane was glad to be back in the routine again, but he found he was very uneasy. He realized that he would feel this way until something was settled concerning Lee Jorms. Martha noticed his restlessness and spoke to him about it.

"Lane, I know this is wearing on you," she said. "If only we knew where he is and what he's doing. Why don't you go and ask Sheriff Cantwell what he thinks about it?"

"Mom, if he knew anything about it, he would come out and tell us," said Lane.

"Yes, I suppose that's true," she said. "But, Lane, what are you going to do? You can't go on like this."

"Do we have a choice?" he asked. "You can't fight something if you don't know what you're fighting."

Another month went by and it was now well into fall. On the first Sunday in October, Lane made arrangements with Elaine for their Sunday afternoon ride. His fears had eased somewhat, since he had heard nothing about Jorms's whereabouts. He picked Elaine up at the appointed time and they headed once more for Sentinel Rock.

"I noticed in church that Callie is just about her old self again," said Elaine.

"Yes, she's well on the way back," said Lane. "I still shudder when I think how close we came to losing her."

"Lane, that was terrible," said Elaine. "Is all this finished now?"

"I wish I could tell you that I know for sure that it is,"

said Lane. "We haven't heard anything of that Jorms for quite a while, but that doesn't mean anything; he could show up at any time."

When they arrived at Sentinel Rock, they sat in their usual places. It was a very peaceful scene, with the sun very warm and clouds floating overhead.

"Lane, I hate to tell you this, but Dad found tracks out by our watering trough the other day," said Elaine. "He's afraid it's that evil man again."

"Now that scares me no end," said Lane. "We were hoping he had left these parts, but it looks like we'll have to be extra careful. Honey, please don't go riding anywhere alone until this thing is settled."

"You don't have to worry about that," she said. "Dad says the same thing."

"Let's think of something more pleasant," said Lane, "like me kissing you." He took her in his arms and their lips met. He then held her close, and she clung to him.

"Honey, since this thing happened to Callie, and we came so close to losing her, it made me realize how uncertain life is; that, in turn, made me realize how much you mean to me," said Lane.

"Oh, Lane, I've been so frightened for fear something would happen to you!" said Elaine. "I love you so much, I couldn't—"

A jeering voice broke in on what she was saying, "Well, now ain't this just hunky-dory. Lucky I just happened along to see this touching scene."

They both whirled around to see Lee Jorms standing behind them with drawn pistol, pointed at Lane. "Well, it looks like my payday has finally come!" he jeered.

"Honey, I'm sorry I was so careless," said Lane.

"You're not half as sorry as you're going to be," said Jorms. "Buster, nobody does to me what you did and gets away with it. I'm going to plug you in the guts so you'll die slow, and then the little lady and me is going for a ride."

"You may kill me, Jorms, but your days are numbered," said Lane. "If you bother this girl in any way, you'll be hunted down like a mad dog."

"You can't scare me, sonny boy. Get ready to say your prayers," said Jorms, raising his gun.

Elaine screamed as he prepared to fire. Startled, he paused for a moment. He then raised his gun once more.

"Drop the gun, Lee!" blared a voice from the bushes nearby.

Jorms whirled around to see where the voice came from.

"I mean it, Lee," said the speaker, now stepping into plain view. It was Val Jorms, with his rifle leveled at his brother.

"Val, what's the matter with you?" yelled Lee. "This is your brother, Lee, who took care of you all those years when we ran away from home. Now drop the gun, and let's get finished here and ride off."

"No, Lee, you're not going to kill anybody," said Val. "There's been too much hatred and killing; it's destroying you. I heard you tell Streeter you were going to kill him and then ride off with this girl. Well, it's not going to happen, so just drop the gun."

Lee paused for a moment, as though undecided. He shrugged as though resigned to do it Val's way, then suddenly spun and snapped a shot at Val. Val's rifle cracked and his brother gasped and dropped his gun.

"You shot me!" He shuddered and slowly crumpled to the ground. Val, crying, dropped his rifle and hurried to his side.

"Lee, Lee, you gave me no choice!" he sobbed.

Lane moved over and put his hand on Val's shoulder.

"He's dead; I killed my own brother," Val said, brokenly.

"And saved my life by doing so," said Lane. "Val, you're quite a man. We can never thank you enough."

"Will you help me get him on his horse?" asked Val. "He's tied over in the bushes; I've been following him for days."

Lane went over and found Jorms's horse. He untied him and led him back to Val. Lane picked up Lee Jorms, draped him across the saddle, and tied him there.

"Are you taking him to town, Val?" asked Lane.

"No, I'm going to take him out and just bury him," said Val. "Would you do me a favor? Tell the sheriff what has happened and that there will be no further trouble."

"I sure will, Val, and thanks again," said Lane. "Val, one more thing: if you're ever around these parts again, stop in; we'll be glad to see you."

Val with tears in his eyes, mounted his horse and took the reins of Lee's mount and rode off. Lane and Elaine watched him until he was out of sight. They got into the buggy and started for home. They were silent for some time.

"Lane, is the danger now over?" finally asked Elaine.

"Honey, this present danger is past," said Lane. "Do you know, Aunt Abby is a pretty smart lady."

"What do you mean, Lane, in what way?" asked Elaine.

"She told me some time ago that we would cry in the tomorrows of our lives, and we have," said Lane. "Well, even though this problem is now over, others will crop up and we will cry some more. That's what life is all about. Together, we can face it; we will laugh in the good times and cry when we have to, but, all in all, it makes for a pretty good life. I'm glad I have you with me so we can face it together. Are you game to start living it?"

Her answer was to drop her head on his shoulder, and to kiss him lightly on the cheek.